The Chef's Surprise Baby

BRENDA HARLEN

HARLEQUIN
SPECIAL
EDITION

HARLEQUIN®
SPECIAL
EDITION™

Recycling programs
for this product may
not exist in your area.

ISBN-13: 978-1-335-40799-3

The Chef's Surprise Baby

Copyright © 2021 by Brenda Harlen

This edition published by arrangement with Harlequin Books S.A.

For questions and comments about the quality of this book,
please contact us at CustomerService@Harlequin.com.

Harlequin Enterprises ULC
22 Adelaide St. West, 40th Floor
Toronto, Ontario M5H 4E3, Canada
www.Harlequin.com

Printed in U.S.A.

Brenda Harlen is a former attorney who once had the privilege of appearing before the Supreme Court of Canada. The practice of law taught her a lot about the world and reinforced her determination to become a writer—because in fiction, she could promise a happy ending! Now she is an award-winning, RITA® Award–nominated nationally bestselling author of more than fifty titles for Harlequin. You can keep up-to-date with Brenda on Facebook and Twitter, or through her website, brendaharlen.com.

Books by Brenda Harlen

Harlequin Special Edition

Match Made in Haven

One Night with the Cowboy
A Chance for the Rancher
The Marine's Road Home
Meet Me Under the Mistletoe
The Rancher's Promise
The Chef's Surprise Baby

Montana Mavericks: What Happened to Beatrix?

A Cowboy's Christmas Carol

Montana Mavericks: Six Brides for Six Brothers

Maverick Christmas Surprise

Montana Mavericks: The Lonelyhearts Ranch

Bring Me a Maverick for Christmas!

Visit the Author Profile page
at Harlequin.com for more titles.

For Tomolynn Torrance
(03 Dec. 1950–29 Nov. 2020)
whose recipes I cherish almost as much
as the memories of our friendship.

Dear Reader,

Welcome back to Haven, Nevada—and into the kitchen at The Home Station restaurant, where executive chef Kyle Landry creates palate-pleasing dishes for even the most discerning customers.

"Friends to lovers" has always been one of my favorite romantic tropes, and "secret babies" another, so it was a lot of fun for me to incorporate both of those story lines into *The Chef's Surprise Baby*. Writing a character who is a chef also required a lot of hands-on research, but my family was happy to reap the benefits of *that* labor! :))

Part-time waitress and web designer Erin Napper impulsively offers to cook a celebratory dinner for her sister and her new husband—who happens to be Erin's ex! The problem? She can't cook! Lucky for Erin, one of her best friends is a culinary wizard.

Kyle is confident that he can help Erin put together a simple meal. But working side by side in her cozy kitchen unexpectedly turns up the heat of attraction between the two friends. One sweet kiss leads to steamy passion...until a family emergency calls Erin home to Arkansas the next day.

A year later, when Erin finally returns to Haven, she has a three-month-old baby in tow.

As the onetime lovers attempt to coparent together, will these conflicting desires be a recipe for disaster? Or for happily-ever-after?

I hope you enjoy reading Kyle and Erin's story as much as I enjoyed writing—and researching—it!

All the best,

Brenda Harlen

"The barely-a-kiss that was interrupted by the untimely arrival of the newlyweds?"

She gave a jerky nod.

"And you think that was intended as a distraction?"

She stared at the wine in her glass. "I can't think of any other reason that you'd kiss me."

"How about the fact that you're a smart and beautiful woman and, after six years, I finally decided to stop ignoring the attraction that's been simmering between us?"

Erin swallowed another mouthful of wine to moisten her suddenly dry throat.

"I guess that could be an alternative explanation," she finally acknowledged.

"It's the truth," Kyle said.

"Now I wish Alanna and Nick had shown up at least thirty seconds later."

"Why thirty seconds?" he asked.

"I figure that's how long it would take for me to know how it feels to really be kissed by you."

"It would take a lot longer than that."

She lowered her feet to the ground and set her wineglass on the coffee table, then sidled closer to him. "Show me."

* * *

MATCH MADE IN HAVEN:
Where gold rush meets gold bands

Chapter One

"Erin—can you hang around for a minute, please?"

Though Kyle Landry had made the request in the form of a question—and even added the word "please"—Erin Napper knew a command when she heard one. And when the executive chef of The Home Station restaurant in Haven, Nevada, asked any of his employees for a moment of their time, they gave it to him.

Especially when the chef and employee in question happened to be good friends.

As a server, Erin primarily worked the front of the house, but Kyle expected his waitstaff to assist with basic prep tasks. He believed that the increased contact between servers and cooks when they were cutting bar garnishes or chopping salad ingredients led to greater camaraderie.

It was often a challenge to work with an exacting and demanding chef, but Erin sincerely enjoyed her job at The Home Station. Besides, who wouldn't love a job that came with free meals every day?

She only worked part-time at the restaurant, to supplement the income she earned as a website designer, but Kyle insisted that she was always welcome at the "family meal"—the staff dinner shared before service. She also frequently got leftovers delivered to her door by the chef himself—a perk afforded to Erin as a result of the fact that they lived in the same building, and maybe because Kyle knew her culinary abilities were so limited that she often opted to eat cold cereal for dinner rather than cook.

But she had yet another reason for hanging around in response to his directive: she owed him an explanation for her screw-ups tonight.

He waited until the rest of the staff had gone before he folded his arms over his chest and leaned back against a gleaming stainless steel counter. Erin had never been a big fan of reality TV cooking shows and certainly wasn't turned on by a temperamental chef in traditional coat and toque. And yet, she couldn't deny that Kyle looked damn good in his uniform.

He also looked like a man in complete command of his domain, because he was. Though only thirty-five, he'd earned his lofty position by committing himself, one hundred percent, to his craft. He had the patience to finesse a delicate beurre blanc sauce and the strength to effortlessly butcher thick slabs of meat. And Erin also knew that every dish she carried out of his kitchen contained a little bit of his heart and soul. More than once over the years, she'd found herself wondering if he poured as much passion into everything he did—and certain that, if he did, a woman would be very lucky to be invited to his bedroom.

"I'd say 'spill,' but it's obvious that happened already," Kyle said, his gaze on the smear of cabernet reduction on the front of the white tuxedo-style shirt she wore tucked into a black pencil skirt protected by a half bistro apron. "So I'll just ask, what was going on with you tonight? You delivered orders to the wrong tables—twice."

She dropped her gaze to the dark slate tile floor. "I know. I'm sorry."

"I didn't ask for an apology. I asked what was going on. You're one of the best on this team. Is everything all right?"

There wasn't any point in hiding the truth—especially not when she'd already decided to ask for his help. But she'd hoped to ease into the subject on her own time and her own terms, not because she'd messed up during service.

"I got a call from my sister before I came in to work," she finally confided.

"Is everything okay at home?" he asked.

Though the chef demanded that his employees demonstrate the same commitment and dedication that he did, he also cared about the people who worked in his restaurant. He willingly juggled schedules to accommodate outside responsibilities and regularly inquired about the well-being of not just his staff but also their families.

"Everything's okay at home," she said. "The problem is *here*—or will be soon."

"And what is that problem?" he asked, sounding curious now.

"Anna and Nick are coming to Haven next week."

"Your sister and your ex-boyfriend," he noted, proving that he did listen when she talked.

"Actually, there's been a change in their status," Erin told him, still not entirely sure how she felt about that change. "Now they're husband and wife."

His brows lifted. "Excuse me? They got *married*?"

She nodded. "This afternoon."

"And you weren't invited to the wedding?"

"They eloped to Vegas."

A revelation that had surprised Erin, because she'd never imagined that her little sister would forgo the opportunity to walk down the aisle in a long white dress and celebrate her nuptials with a big, fancy wedding. Since the day she was born—twenty-eight years earlier, on Erin's third birthday—Anna had been the center of attention in the Napper family and now considered the spotlight her due.

Which, of course, made Erin wonder about the reason for their low-key ceremony. Was it possible that the bride had realized an elaborate family celebration would be awkward for the sister who'd lost her virginity to the groom nearly fifteen years earlier?

"Is she pregnant?" Kyle asked now.

"What?" That was a possibility that hadn't occurred to Erin. "No!"

He held her gaze steadily. "Are you sure?"

No, but she was fairly certain that Anna would have told her if she was.

Wouldn't she?

She pushed her doubts aside.

"My sister has her faults," she noted, "but being careless isn't one of them."

"So why the urgency to exchange vows?" he wondered.

"She said they didn't want to wait to start their life together," Erin said.

"And how do you feel about that?"

"I'm trying to be okay with it," she said. "I mean, they've been dating for more than six months, so it's not like I haven't had time to get used to the fact that they're together."

But Nick Burnett had been Erin's first boyfriend. Her first love. Even if she'd been the one who'd decided to end their relationship when she went away to school. At the time, he'd claimed that she'd shattered his heart beyond repair, but she'd always known that he'd find someone else. And maybe she should be happy that he'd done so—she just wished that someone was anyone other than her own sister.

"Nick and I broke up a long time ago," she continued. "It's just weird, you know? To think about my ex-boyfriend and my sister…together. Married."

"So that's what mixed up your service tonight," he realized.

"Actually…it was the prime rib au jus with roasted fingerling potatoes and glazed baby carrots that got me thinking about my menu."

"Your menu?" he echoed.

She lifted her shoulders. "When Anna said that they were coming to Haven before heading home to Silver Hook, I invited them for dinner. Of course, I was planning to order pizza from Jo's, but then she made a snarky remark about me not knowing how to cook, which of course made me want to prove her wrong."

"But…you don't know how to cook," Kyle reminded her, not unkindly.

"Lucky for me, *you* do," she said.

He shook his head. "Oh no. You're not dragging me into the middle of this family drama."

"There's not going to be any drama," she promised. "I just need you to cook a simple meal that Anna and Nick would believe I made."

"No," he said again.

Erin wasn't ready to throw in her cards—not when she had an ace up her sleeve. "Do you remember when you were just a line cook at Diggers', desperate to prove to Liam Gilmore that you could be the chef he needed for this restaurant?"

"Of course, I do," he agreed, his tone wary.

"You offered to prepare a sample of menu items—to show him what you were capable of. But you couldn't do all the prepping and cooking and serving on your own, so you asked a friend for help."

"I remember that, too," he acknowledged. "I also remember thanking that friend—and later getting her a job in the same restaurant so that she would earn much better tips than she ever got serving pizzas at Jo's or lunch specials at Diggers'."

It was a valid point, Erin acknowledged to herself, but not one that dissuaded her from pressing her case.

"You also said that you owed her one, and if she ever needed a favor, all she had to do was ask… So I'm asking, Kyle. *Please*."

"Do you really want to lie to your sister and brother-in-law?"

"I agree it's not ideal," she said. "But after backing myself into a corner, what choice do I have?"

He hesitated for a moment before saying, "I could teach you how to cook."

She laughed. She couldn't help it. The idea was just too outrageous for her to believe it was a sincere offer.

"You don't think I'm up to the challenge?" he asked.

"It's not your abilities as a teacher that I doubt, but mine as a student," she told him.

"You're a smart, capable woman, Erin. I don't think there's anything you can't do if you put your mind to it."

His words filled her with pleasure—and more than a little bit of trepidation. "But…they're going to be here in three days."

He grinned. "Then we don't have any time to waste."

* * *

As Kyle made his way toward Erin's apartment the next morning, he acknowledged that she was right—he did owe her. And every day that he walked into the kitchen at The Home Station—*his* kitchen—he was aware of that fact. He owed Liam Gilmore, too, for being willing to take a chance on him. But he felt confident that he'd repaid that debt by creating an innovative menu and preparing hearty meals that managed to satisfy the hungry rancher as much as they impressed the sophisticated traveler.

Prior to the opening of The Home Station, Haven residents had to go out of town for upscale dining. Now people from Elko and Battle Mountain—and other locations even further out—came to Haven to eat, and many of them became repeat customers, happy to travel the distance for a delicious meal—often followed by a comfortable bed at the newly remodeled Stagecoach Inn.

Almost everyone Kyle knew had dined at The Home Station at least once, and reservations were typically booked months in advance. The first customers had been drawn by curiosity, many of them determined to proclaim that the new restaurant wasn't anything special or different and certainly wouldn't last. Between the all-day breakfast menu at Sunnyside Diner, the legendary pizza at Jo's and the more extensive but casual offerings at Diggers' Bar & Grill, there were already enough options for local dining. Those same customers inevitably left The Home Station appreciating that they'd enjoyed a culinary experience that was so much more than a plate of food.

The only local resident he personally knew who'd stubbornly refused to come in for a meal was his own mother. Three years after the restaurant opened, Jolene Landry had yet to forgive Kyle for choosing to work in a stranger's kitchen rather than hers.

It had been easier for Kyle to forgive his mom for forcing him to make that choice, because he was happy at The Home Station. And his sister was happy, because Lucy was now the heir apparent to the pizzeria. But Jo continued to believe—or at least pretended to believe—that one day Kyle would suddenly discover that he missed making pizzas, give his notice to Liam Gilmore and return to Jo's.

So yeah, when Erin said that family relationships were complicated, he understood. And that was why he was prepared to teach her to cook, though he had no doubt it would be easier for both of them if she let him prepare the meal for her sister and new brother-in-law.

He balanced one of the paper to-go cups from The Daily Grind on top of the other and knocked on her door. Then again, louder. He was about to knock a third time when it was finally wrenched open from the other side.

"Do you have any idea what time it is?" Erin demanded, looking obviously unhappy—and recently awakened.

"Not exactly," he admitted. "But it's got to be

close to nine, because it was eight thirty when I was at The Daily Grind."

"It's too early, whatever o'clock it is," she grumbled. "I was up until four working on updates for a client's website."

"How was I supposed to know that?" he asked, offering her one of the cups.

"You could have texted to see if it was okay for you to stop by at this hour."

"I did text," he pointed out. "You didn't reply."

"Because I was sleeping."

Which he'd already guessed on the basis of her attire: a pair of pink plaid boxer shorts with a skimpy pink tank top. There was also a crease on her cheek from her pillowcase and her long blond hair was sexily tousled, making him think that a man who woke up beside her wouldn't be in any hurry to get out of her bed—

And where had *that* thought come from?

He cleared his throat along with his mind. "Drink your coffee," he suggested. "Then we'll chat."

"Here's a better idea—I'll go back to sleep for another three hours and *then* we'll chat."

He shook his head. "I have to be at the restaurant in three hours." He glanced at the Tissot watch on his wrist, a graduation present from his mom and a symbol of her pride in what he'd accomplished and her belief in his future—when she'd believed that his future was at Jo's Pizza. "Actually, less than that now."

Erin peeled back the tab on the lid and cautiously sipped the hot liquid.

"You said your sister and her husband are coming…when?" Kyle prompted.

"Please," she implored. "I need at least three minutes for the caffeine to hit my brain before I can be expected to have a conversation."

"Do you think maybe you could get dressed in those three minutes?" he asked. "Or at least grab a robe?"

"You don't get to show up at my door before nine o'clock on a Sunday morning and be offended that I'm in my pajamas," she said.

"I'm not offended," he told her. But he was inching close to being aroused, and that was dangerous territory for their relationship. "You just look a little… um…cold."

He'd been trying really hard not to notice that the tight peaks of her nipples were pressing against the thin fabric of her top, but his eyes were clearly not accepting the commands from his brain, because his gaze kept dropping to her chest. And when he managed to lift it to her face again now, he saw that her cheeks were a darker shade of pink than the skimpy top that clung to her breasts.

"I'll get dressed," she decided. "But I'm taking my coffee with me."

He nodded as she turned to go, failing again in his efforts not to notice that the hem of those shorts barely covered the sweet curve of her butt—and that she had really great legs.

Obviously he'd been too long without a woman if he was ogling a friend, he decided, and she deserved better than that. He swallowed another mouthful of his own coffee and nearly scalded his throat in the process, no doubt punishment for his inappropriate thoughts.

Erin and his sister had been roommates at the University of Texas and remained in close contact after graduation, though Kyle didn't meet Erin until she came to Haven for Lucy's wedding. There had been a hint of a spark in the beginning, but when he'd realized the sexy stranger's connection to his sister, he'd ruthlessly extinguished it. Not just because he knew that Lucy wouldn't approve and he didn't want to be the cause of any more friction in his family, but also because any kind of romantic entanglement— no matter how temporary—with someone he might cross paths with again at family events was a complication he didn't want.

A smart decision, as it turned out, because Erin's visit to town for the wedding had resulted in her moving to Haven only a few months later. In the six years that had passed since then, Kyle and Erin had gotten to know one another a lot better and become good friends themselves. And while he'd never lost sight of the fact that she was a beautiful woman, he'd also never been tempted to make a move that would jeopardize their friendship.

Because as much as Kyle appreciated and enjoyed female companionship, his track record with relationships was abysmal. The biggest barrier to success was always his demanding work schedule. While there were plenty of women who liked the idea of dating a chef, none of them—or at least none that he'd gone out with—had understood that being in charge of a kitchen required him to be *in* the kitchen. Which meant that he worked every Friday and Saturday night and every major holiday, and stealing away for a romantic weekend wasn't likely to ever happen.

Mikayla, a court clerk and his most recent ex, claimed to understand that his job required him to work weekends—but she'd been certain he didn't mean *every* weekend. Of course, she worked eight-to-four Monday through Friday, and she'd started to resent that he was always at work when she got home and that they could never go away for a few days—or even a single Saturday night—because he was needed at the restaurant. After five months of dating—mostly late evenings, when the restaurant closed early, or Saturday mornings, before he went in to work—she'd decided that she wanted more than a few hours a week with someone who was too selfish and self-centered to appreciate everything she was offering.

He hadn't dated another woman since she walked out the door. He simply didn't have it in him to disappoint anyone else.

And the absolute last person he'd ever want to disappoint was Erin, which was just one more reason he had to forget how temptingly sexy she'd looked in those skimpy pj's.

Easier said than done, he suspected.

Chapter Two

"Are you happy now?" Erin asked, returning to the living room, where Kyle had settled with his coffee on her plum-colored leather sofa.

Despite his earlier admonition to himself, he let his gaze skim over her again, from her head to her feet. She'd brushed the tangles out of her hair so that it fell like a curtain of silk over her shoulders, and her toenails were painted a pretty shade of pink that might have matched her pj's, if he'd been able to tear his gaze from her skimpy attire to notice her toes earlier. She'd also donned a simple scoop-neck T-shirt in a bluish-green color that somehow made her eyes look even bluer, along with a pair of navy capri-style pants.

"I'm always happy," he said, responding to her

question before countering with his own. "Are you awake now?"

"Barely," she admitted, perching onto the arm of a chair across from him. "But the coffee is helping, so thank you for that."

"You're welcome." He lifted his own cup to his lips and swallowed another mouthful.

"Now are you going to tell me why you were at my door before nine a.m.?" she asked.

"Because I couldn't remember when you said your sister and brother-in-law were coming to town."

"Wednesday."

"Then we'd better figure out what you want to cook so that I can give you a list of ingredients to pick up before our first lesson this afternoon."

"You want to start *today*?"

"It's not about want but need." He winked. "Because a woman who can set off the fire alarm making a grilled cheese sandwich is going to need more than one lesson."

"That happened *once*," she said, her tone defensive. "Because I was making lunch while also answering emails and got distracted. And while it was admittedly embarrassing, the incident did lead to a date with a hunky firefighter who responded to the call."

Then she sighed. "Of course, that relationship ended eight months later when he finally accepted that I really couldn't cook."

"Everyone can cook," he insisted. "You just need someone to teach you the basics."

But she was nibbling on her bottom lip—a telltale sign of nerves—and he realized that she had sincere doubts about whether she was up to the task.

He didn't share her concerns, because she'd proven that she could tackle any goal or challenge that she set for herself. He also knew that her struggles in the kitchen were less a reflection of her skills than they were a commentary on her relationship with her mother, who'd never spent any time in the kitchen with Erin. But the fact that his friend had never before shown any interest in putting together a real meal made him ask, "Is this guy really worth the effort?"

"Are you talking about Seth?" she asked, naming the firefighter ex-boyfriend.

He shook his head. "No. I'm talking about the ex who's now married to your sister."

She frowned. "You think I'm doing this for Nick?"

"Aren't you?"

"No." Her response was immediate and vehement enough to convince him that she believed it to be true. "I'm doing this to show both Anna *and* Nick that I'm totally okay with their relationship."

"If you were totally okay with their relationship, you wouldn't be trying so hard," Kyle pointed out.

"It's just a little…weird," she said. "If not really surprising."

"Because your sister's always wanted everything that you had?" he guessed.

"And she always got it."

She didn't sound resentful as much as resigned,

and Kyle suddenly remembered a story she'd told him a few years earlier, about her mom asking her to give up a favorite Christmas gift to Anna because she liked Erin's toy better than the one she'd received. From the time her sister was old enough to say "I want," Erin was encouraged to "be a big girl" and share with Anna.

"But I'm looking forward to her visit," Erin said, and even managed to sound as if she believed it. "I haven't seen anyone from home since Christmas."

"You couldn't wait to get back after your trip to Silver Hook in December," he reminded her.

It was true, Erin acknowledged, if only to herself.

And part of the reason was that it was while she was home for the holidays that she'd discovered her sister was dating her ex-boyfriend—and no one had thought to give her a heads-up about the fact. Only Roger, her brother Owen's partner, had expressed any remorse that Erin had obviously been ambushed by the news of Anna's relationship with Nick. Of course, Roger and Owen lived in Portland, so they'd been as in the dark as Erin until Nick showed up for the family gathering on Christmas Eve. Her oldest brother, Ian, and sister-in-law, Marissa, had no such excuse. Or maybe they'd assumed that she wouldn't care—and she didn't.

But she would have appreciated a little bit of warning.

"So...menu," she said, steering the topic of conversation back around again. "I was thinking Italian."

"How about chicken parmesan with spaghetti?"

"One of my favorites." She swiped the screen on her cell phone to open her memo pad tab and create a grocery list. "Tell me what I need to get."

Kyle was organizing the ingredients Erin had set out on the counter when her cell phone rang.

She glanced at the display and exhaled a weary sigh.

"Are you going to get that?" Kyle asked, when she made no move to do so.

"It's my mom."

"Which doesn't answer my question," he noted.

"We had our regularly scheduled phone call Wednesday morning," she told him. "I can't imagine why she'd be calling me now."

"You might find out why if you answer the phone," he suggested, sounding amused.

"But we're in the middle of cooking."

"We're not in the middle," he denied. "We haven't even started."

She sighed again and swiped a finger over the screen to connect the call. "Hello?"

"Erin?"

They went through the same routine every time Bonnie called, despite the fact that no one else ever answered Erin's phone. "Yes, Mom, it's me."

"How are you?"

She gave her usual response. "I'm fine, thanks. How are you doing?"

"Good."

"How's Dad?" she asked, conscious of the fact

that Kyle was only a few feet away, able to hear every word of her end of the typically awkward conversation.

"Good," Bonnie said again.

"Anything new in Silver Hook?" Erin prompted, because she was certain there had to be a reason for this unexpected Sunday afternoon call.

"Good."

The distracted response gave Erin pause. "Is everything okay?"

"Oh, yes. Um… Of course."

"Are you sure?" she pressed. "You sound a little preoccupied."

"I'm sorry," Bonnie apologized. "I was just checking my email."

"I'd apologize for interrupting, but you called me," Erin reminded her.

"I just wanted to check in, to see how you're doing."

"I'm fine," she said again.

"And…I wanted to let you know that Anna and Nick got married," her mother continued.

"I heard."

"How…? Who…?"

"Anna called me yesterday," Erin told her. "After the wedding."

"Oh." Bonnie obviously hadn't anticipated this revelation. "Well, I hope you were able to congratulate your sister."

"Of course. I offered them my best wishes."

"I'm glad. I know this can't be easy for you."

"It really doesn't have anything to do with me."

"You've always tried to be so brave—"

"Nothing about this situation requires bravery," Erin interjected to assure her. "If they're happy, then I'm happy for them."

"But you seemed…upset…to realize they were together at Christmas."

"I was surprised," she said. "More so that nobody bothered to tell me than by the fact that they were dating."

"Anna worried about telling you… She thought you might still be in love with Nick."

"We broke up more than twelve years ago," she reminded her mother.

"A woman never forgets her first love," Bonnie said knowingly.

"Speaking of," Erin said, desperate to change the topic, "is Dad around?"

"Actually, he's not at the moment."

"He's out fishing," she guessed, only a little disappointed. It was always a pleasure to talk to her dad, but she knew that Kyle was waiting to start her cooking lesson. And while she wasn't quite as eager, she was at least determined to pay attention.

"Every chance he gets," her mom confirmed now. "And we were so busy this weekend, he didn't have a free minute to put his line in the water."

Brian Napper frequently said that he'd been happy to take over his family's fishing resort because it meant he got to spend every day doing what he loved. He hadn't anticipated Sunfish Bay would become so successful that, with each year that passed, he had less and less time to enjoy the simple pleasures.

"When he comes in, be sure to give him a hug and kiss from me and tell him that I love him."

"I will," Bonnie promised.

"And…I love you, too," she said, feeling just a little bit guilty that she'd tacked it on as an afterthought.

"And me, too, you."

An awkward but unsurprising reply that alleviated the slight twinge of guilt.

Kyle had prepared more than a few meals in Erin's kitchen, but usually when he was cooking, his friend and neighbor stayed out of his way, content to sip a glass of wine and watch him work. However, teaching her to cook necessitated working in close proximity, making the already small galley kitchen feel a lot smaller.

The road to a cold shower is paved with good intentions, he suddenly remembered, as Erin squeezed through the narrow space between the island—where he was arranging bowls and utensils—and the counter. Her front brushed against his back as she did so, causing electric sparks to skip and skitter through his veins.

Yep, *way too long* since he'd slept with a woman, Kyle decided. Because that was the only possible reason he was suddenly reacting to Erin's closeness.

She'd pulled her hair into a ponytail to keep it out of the way, but she was wearing the same T-shirt and capris that she'd put on earlier, now with a white butcher-style apron over them to protect her clothes. He'd made her put on shoes, too. Not just because he didn't want to be distracted by her sexy pink toenails but also because bare feet were a potential hazard in the kitchen.

Still, her presence provided him with plenty of other tantalizing distractions, such as the fact that he could smell the subtle, peachy fragrance of her shampoo every time she turned her head—as she seemed to do every two minutes. Or maybe it was a scented body lotion she rubbed over her creamy skin to keep it soft and smooth that he was smelling. And he definitely should *not* be thinking about Erin rubbing lotion over her body, her narrow hands slicking over her skin, tracing the contours and curves—

"How's this?"

Her question jerked him back to the present, and the chicken that she'd pummeled to almost paper thinness.

"You want the breast—" he cleared his throat and hastily amended "—the *chicken* to be of uniform thickness so it cooks evenly. You don't need to be able to see through it.

"But that's my fault," he acknowledged ruefully. "My mind was wandering."

"Good thing we haven't turned on the heat under the frying pan, or the fire department might be on the way," she teased.

She was right, and he knew better than to allow his thoughts to stray when he was in the kitchen.

Usually.

But he'd never before been in such close confines with a woman he was, suddenly and inexplicably, having trouble remembering was off-limits.

He and Erin had been friends for half a dozen years—why was he only now noticing how good she smelled? Or that those capri pants hugged her sweetly shaped bottom? And that her lips, shiny with gloss, were plump and perfectly shaped for kissing?

The truth, of course, was that he wasn't only now noticing. That he'd felt the initial stirrings of attraction the first time he saw her. But he'd pushed those feelings aside—successfully—for more than six years.

So why was he struggling to continue to do so now?

"Now you're going to dip the chicken in the beaten egg," he said, refocusing on the task at hand.

She picked up the chicken.

"I usually use a fork," he said. "But fingers work as well. Just make sure you wash thoroughly after handling raw poultry."

She dropped the chicken into the egg with a splash. "You didn't say to use a fork."

"You're right," he agreed.

She went to the sink to wash her hands.

While she was doing that, he turned on the element under the pan to heat the oil.

After soaping up and rinsing and drying her hands, Erin took a fork from the cutlery drawer and stabbed the chicken with the tines to lift it out of the egg mixture.

"Now transfer it to the bread crumbs and coat it

evenly, using the fork to press the crumbs into the chicken."

She followed his directions precisely, confirming his suspicion that she wasn't actually a bad cook but had simply never been taught. As a result of her strained relationship with her mom, Erin had spent more time with her dad while she was growing up. Which explained why she knew how to bait a hook and gut a fish but not how to pan fry the fillets.

She was a good student, eager to do everything just right. And she looked not just earnest but sexy in the apron she'd donned to protect her clothes from spatters—though he imagined she'd look even sexier wearing nothing but the apron.

A thought he forced himself to tamp down on. *Again.*

Two days later, Erin paced the short distance between the kitchen and the front door, peeking at the clock on the stove every time she completed a lap.

What had she been thinking, inviting Kyle for dinner?

He was a world-class chef and she was a website designer with a freezer full of microwavable meals.

But under his tutelage, she'd done a decent job with the chicken parm on her first run-through, if she did say so herself. Then she'd made it again on her own the next day, carefully following every step of his precise, handwritten directions. Still, she'd wanted to do another test run, to ensure that she'd feel confident about preparing the same meal for Anna and Nick.

Thankfully, Kyle knew her well enough that she could trust his expectations wouldn't be too high. No doubt he'd consider himself lucky if he didn't get food poisoning. The bigger mistake had been in offering to cook for her sister and brother-in-law.

Was she trying too hard to prove that she was okay with their marriage? And who was she proving it to? Neither Anna nor Nick had seemed the least bit concerned about Erin's reaction to their relationship when she was home for Christmas, and why would they be? It had nothing to do with her.

Whatever romantic feelings she'd once had for Nick had fizzled away a long time ago. Sure, she had happy memories of the times they'd spent together, but those times were in the past—Anna and Nick were the present and future.

Okay, maybe she was a tiny bit envious that they'd managed to make the kind of romantic connection that had thus far eluded her. And maybe she was a little sad to consider the possibility that she might never make that connection with someone. Not that she was ready to throw in the towel at the age of thirty-one, because she was certain that she had a lot of good years ahead of her. Except that if the years behind were any indication, she shouldn't get her hopes up, either. Because despite having dated a lot of great guys, she hadn't been able to imagine spending the rest of her life with any one of them.

Truth be told, the longest relationship she'd had

in the past several years was with Kyle, and the only reason that one had endured was that they were simply friends with no expectations of anything more. Well, if she was being perfectly honest, there had been occasional moments when she'd found herself wondering *what if...*

What if she snuggled up to him when they were watching TV on a rainy Sunday afternoon after brunch service at the restaurant?

What if she held on to his arm when they walked home together after closing the restaurant late on a Friday night?

What if she leaned forward and touched her lips to his mouth instead of his cheek when she thanked him for dropping off dinner for her?

What if she made a move and ruined everything?

It was the last *what if* that held her back from chancing any of the other scenarios.

That, and the fact that Kyle had never given any indication that he saw her as anything more than a friend.

Not until he'd shown up at her door early Sunday morning and caught her in her pj's, and she'd caught a glimpse of something that might have been interest in his gaze.

Or maybe her sleep-deprived brain had imagined it.

In any event, that glimpse had been the beginning and the end of it. He'd been a consummate professional the whole time they'd worked side by side. Not just appropriate in his behavior but diligent in his teaching, because she'd actually managed to turn out something that tasted like chicken parmesan.

Of course, he'd been instructing and encouraging every step of the way, but she'd done the work. And he'd been proud of her—he'd even told her so, his words bolstering her shaky confidence.

And if she'd felt her body temperature rise in the close confines of her kitchen, it was obviously a one-sided awareness that warmed only *her* blood, made only *her* skin tingle whenever they touched, and fueled only *her* nighttime fantasies.

She jolted at the knock on the door, despite the fact that she'd been waiting for it.

"You're right on time," she said, ushering Kyle through the apartment and into the kitchen.

"I wouldn't dare be late and risk spoiling the meal you've prepared," he said.

She was grateful for that—all too aware that he'd had to entrust the restaurant kitchen to his staff while he slipped away for a short while, just because she asked.

"I appreciate your willingness to be my guinea pig," she said, plating the food she'd prepared and setting it in front of him.

He waited for her to sit down across from him before he picked up his knife and fork. There was a slight furrow between his brows as he scrutinized her culinary offering.

"The chicken is a good, uniform thickness," he said. "But why is it round?"

"Because it's not chicken," she told him. "It's eggplant."

"Were you sick of chicken? Or was there another reason you decided to change the menu?" he asked curiously.

"I got a text from my sister last night," she explained. "'FYI, in case Mom didn't tell you, I'm a vegetarian now.'"

"Now?" he echoed. "Does that mean she stopped eating meat sometime between Saturday afternoon, when she told you they were coming to Haven, and last night?"

Erin shook her head. "Apparently it was part of her New Year's resolution to live a healthier lifestyle."

"I haven't even met your sister and already I don't like her," he said.

"Because she doesn't eat meat?"

"Because she's obviously so spoiled that she expects everyone to indulge her whims."

"I don't think that vegetarianism is a whim," she felt compelled to argue in her sister's defense.

But she couldn't deny that Anna was spoiled, even if her little sister's expectations were simply a consequence of her experience.

"At least she's not vegan," she said now, "so I didn't have to worry about cutting the dairy ingredients."

"Life wouldn't be worth living without butter," Kyle said sincerely, as he cut into his eggplant.

Erin's gaze followed his fork as it moved from

his plate to his mouth. He chewed slowly, then swallowed, his expression giving nothing away.

"It tastes good," he finally said. "The breading is nice and crisp, and the sauce has good flavor."

"But?" she prompted, because she could hear the unspoken word in his voice.

"The texture of the eggplant is a little...mushy."

She sampled a bite from her own plate. "Ugh. It is mushy."

"A little," he acknowledged.

"Why? What did I do wrong?" She didn't try to disguise the frustration in her voice.

"Did you sweat the eggplant?" he asked.

"I sweated while cooking the eggplant," she said.

Kyle shook his head, but a smile tugged at the corners of his mouth. "Sweating just means you salt the veg to draw out the excess moisture before cooking."

"The recipe didn't say anything about sweating," she protested.

"It's not always necessary," he said. "But it's a step that, sometimes, if you skip it, results in mushy eggplant."

She dropped her fork onto her plate and pushed it aside, her appetite lost. "Why did I ever think I could do this?"

"Because you can do anything you put her mind to," he told her.

"Clearly not."

"This is just a little bump in the road," he assured her.

"They're coming *tomorrow*." She dropped her

head into her hands. "Maybe I should order a vegetarian lasagna from Diggers'."

"Before you do that, maybe you could take out the knife between my shoulder blades?"

His outraged tone made her smile, just a little. "I know you could make a better vegetarian lasagna," she acknowledged. "But you've already done so much for me."

"I haven't done very much at all," he denied.

She sighed. "I had no idea how much work putting together a single meal would be."

"Cooking is work," he agreed. "But it can also be a joy, feeding the soul as much as the body."

"You can spare me the philosophy—I just wanted to be able to put dinner on the table."

"And you've done that."

"I fed you mushy eggplant." She sighed. "I know I'm making a bigger deal out of this than it needs to be. It's just…"

"It's just what?" he prompted.

"My family always teases me about being a lousy cook, and I want to prove that I'm not."

"You're not a lousy cook," he assured her. "But even if you were—so what? We all have our areas of expertise. Why does it matter if you're not comfortable in the kitchen? Julia Child might have made French cuisine accessible to American audiences, but I bet she couldn't design a website."

"Who's Julia Child?"

He winced at her response even as he shook his

head. "It doesn't matter. What matters is that you have other talents."

"None that are going to feed a husband or child." She sighed again. "*If* I ever get married and have a family of my own."

"So marry a man who can cook," he said, as if it was that easy.

But his suggestion did start her thinking...

"It's too bad we're friends," she teased. "Otherwise, we might be perfect for one another."

Kyle's expression was serious as he held her gaze across the table. "Yeah, it's too bad."

Chapter Three

Once a month, Erin met Lucy for a late breakfast at the Sunnyside Diner. Her college pal had quickly transformed from stranger to best friend when they were assigned a room together, and it was because of Lucy that Erin had first visited the northern Nevada town that was now her home.

A lot had happened in the thirteen years since they were freshmen together—though, if Erin was honest, more in her friend's life than her own. Lucy and Claudio—who were coming up on their seventh anniversary—were essentially running Jo's Pizza, living in a new home they'd had built near the restaurant, were the doting parents of a three-year-old Corgi and enthusiastically working toward adding a human baby to their family.

As a result of being at the pizzeria late almost every night, Lucy was habitually running behind schedule in the mornings, so Erin usually took advantage of the time to catch up on emails and savor a first cup of coffee while she waited. But when she pulled into the parking lot of the diner Wednesday morning, she saw that her friend's SUV was already there.

"Am I late?" she asked, glancing at the time displayed on her phone as she slid onto the vinyl bench seat across from Lucy.

"No," her friend assured her. "I was early for a change."

"Are you sick?" she asked teasingly.

"No. And I'm not pregnant, either," Lucy said, obviously feeling discouraged by a recent negative test result.

"Did you really expect it to happen the first time you guys had unprotected sex?"

"No," her friend admitted. "But I'll bet there are a bunch of teenage girls who didn't think it would happen that way for them, either, only to be proven wrong by two little lines on a stick."

Good point, Erin acknowledged to herself.

"On the plus side, not being pregnant means that you and Claudio get to keep trying," she said, urging her friend to find a silver lining.

"There is that," Lucy agreed, with a small smile.

Erin thanked the server who filled her coffee cup, then topped up Lucy's, too.

"Are you ready to order?" she asked.

"I'll have the Mediterranean omelet today," Lucy said. "With whole wheat toast and a side of sausage."

The server nodded and shifted her attention to Erin.

"The banana pecan pancakes," she decided.

"Bacon or sausage?"

"Both, please."

"Bacon *and* sausage?" Lucy said, when the server had moved on. "You must be hungry this morning."

"I'm cooking a vegetarian meal for dinner, so I figured I should get my meat quota in early."

"Give me a minute," her friend said, holding up a hand in a universal "stop" gesture. "I'm trying to figure out if I'm more shocked by the vegetarian part or the fact that you're cooking."

Lucy sipped her coffee, considering.

"The cooking," she decided.

"Ha ha," Erin said, unamused.

"I wasn't being funny," her friend remarked. "I know how your relationship with the hunky firefighter started."

She sighed. "I'm never going to live that down, am I?"

"Not in this lifetime," Lucy promised.

"Well, not everyone thinks I'm a disaster in the kitchen."

"Because not everyone has seen you try to crack an egg."

"Kyle assured me that a little bit of shell never hurt anyone."

Lucy paused with her mug halfway to her mouth.

"Has my brother expanded your prep duties at the restaurant?"

"No, he's…um…teaching me how to cook."

Her friend set her coffee down again without drinking. "He's teaching you to cook?"

"He's not trying to turn me into a chef or anything— I mean, he's good, but he's not a miracle worker," Erin said. "He just helped me with some basics."

She smiled her thanks to the server when she delivered their meals—along with a carafe of warm maple syrup for her pancakes.

"I'm surprised he has any time for extracurricular cooking," Lucy mused.

"Not a lot," Erin agreed.

"So…tell me about this vegetarian meal you mentioned."

Erin poured syrup over her pancakes. "Eggplant parmesan with spaghetti."

"Actually, I'm more interested in the why than the what," her friend said.

"Because my sister and her husband are coming for a visit."

"When did your sister get married?"

"She and Nick eloped in Vegas on Saturday."

Lucy sliced off a corner of her omelet. "You know that awkward family gathering you endured at Christmas? I see a lot more of those in your future," she predicted.

"It wasn't really so awkward," Erin said. "More… unexpected."

"So…how far along is she?" her friend asked curiously.

Erin frowned. "Why does everyone assume a quick wedding means a pregnant bride?"

"Who's everyone?"

"Just you and Kyle," she confided. "But you're the only two people I've told."

"Are you sure that she's not pregnant?" Lucy pressed.

"No," she admitted. "But I can't imagine Anna being careless about birth control."

"There are a lot of reasons that birth control can fail." Lucy poked at a sausage link. "And apparently a lot of reasons that some women don't get pregnant even when they're not using birth control."

"It will happen," Erin said confidently. "I know it will."

"How do you know?"

"Because I can't think of any two people who would make better parents than you and Claudio." She said the words not only to reassure her friend, but also because they were true, and was rewarded with a small smile from Lucy.

"Now, back to your sister and your ex-boyfriend now brother-in-law," she said. "Should we make a bet on when the baby's due?"

Kyle had absolutely no doubts when he was in the kitchen. It was the one place where he knew that he wasn't just in charge but in control. The place where he'd always been the most comfortable.

So why was he leaving the dinner service in the (admittedly more-than-capable) hands of his sous-chef, Giselle Parsons, to join Erin's sure-to-be-awkward family dinner?

It was a question he didn't know how to answer—especially considering that Erin hadn't even invited him to share the meal she was preparing. Because she knew that he worked at the restaurant on Wednesday nights.

And yet here he was, standing outside her apartment, more concerned about Erin than the preparation and presentation of the beef tenderloin with scallops Oscar—one of the restaurant's featured menu items tonight.

But would his presence send the wrong message to his friend?

He wanted only to offer moral support, but now that he was knocking on her door, he worried that Erin might think he didn't trust her to prepare the meal.

She opened the door looking frazzled and sounding breathless. Her eyes registered surprise, then relief, as she stepped back to allow him entry.

"Thank God," she said fervently.

He lifted a brow. "I'm flattered to know that I'm the answer to your prayers."

She rolled her eyes. "When I heard the knock, I thought it was Anna and Nick, and I'm not ready for them to be here."

"What time are you expecting them?" he asked, with a glance at his watch.

"Six," she replied, and then she frowned. "And you should be at the restaurant. What are you doing here?"

"I heard there was eggplant parmesan on the menu tonight and didn't want to miss it," he said.

"Didn't want me to screw it up, you mean?" she guessed. Obviously, despite the trial runs, she was still feeling a little uncertain about the meal she'd prepared.

"I have total faith in you," he assured her.

She managed a smile then, though it quickly faded. "I'm not sure it isn't completely misguided, but thank you."

"And since I'm here—can I give you a hand with anything?" he offered.

"The only things I have left to do are set the table and change my clothes."

"I'll set the table," he said, since he shouldn't be thinking about Erin stripping off the clothes she was wearing. And he definitely shouldn't offer to help with that task—no matter how much he might want to.

"That would be great, but are you sure you wouldn't rather be at The Home Station?"

"Giselle's got everything under control there," he said, because he was confident that his sous-chef could handle anything that came up. And because he'd checked the reservation book to ensure there were no VIPs whose meals would require the head chef's personal attention.

"In that case, I'll say *thank you* and leave you to it," she said, and disappeared down the hall toward her bedroom.

He'd been in her kitchen enough times to know where everything was—he even found her good place mats in the bottom drawer beside the stove. When the dishes and cutlery were in place, he found a corkscrew and opened the bottle of cabernet sauvignon she'd left out on the counter so the wine would have time to breathe before the meal.

"I wasn't sure about the wine," Erin said, joining him in the dining room. "I'm not sure where Anna and Nick are staying tonight, or how far they have to drive to get there. But if we don't have the wine with dinner, I'm definitely going to want a glass—or two or three—afterward."

He chuckled at that, then he turned to face her—and the laughter died in his throat.

She hadn't been gone more than ten minutes, but in that time, she'd effected an impressive transformation. She'd released her hair from its ponytail and replaced her T-shirt and jeans with a sleeveless dress that dipped low in the front—and even lower in the back—and a skirt that swirled several inches above her knees. She'd also added a touch of makeup—mascara that darkened her lashes and gloss that added shine to her lips.

"But thanks for setting the table. It looks great."

"Yes, you do," he said.

Erin blinked. "I'm sorry?" she said, obviously as surprised as he was that he'd said that part out loud.

"You look great," he said again, because it was true.

"Oh. Um. Thanks."

He should have left it at that. The gruffness of

his tone and the awkwardness of her response were clear indications that they were treading on boggy ground. But for some inexplicable reason, instead of retreating, he pushed forward. "You don't wear dresses very often."

"I usually wear a skirt when I work at the restaurant."

"But that's part of your uniform, so it doesn't really count," he said dismissively.

Plus the modest style of her work attire didn't draw attention to her legs the way this dress did. Or maybe it was the wedge-heeled sandals on her feet that ratcheted up the sexy factor.

Thankfully, he managed to keep those thoughts—and his tongue—inside his head.

"I'm not sure I agree with your logic," Erin responded lightly, "but I appreciate the compliment."

He nodded and clamped his jaw shut so that he didn't ask how she could possibly be wearing a bra with a dress that dipped so low in the back—because she probably wasn't, and he didn't need to have that supposition confirmed.

Erin glanced at the silver bangle-style watch on her wrist. "When you knocked on the door, I was worried that they were early. Now I'm worried that they're going to be late."

"Do you want a glass of wine while you're waiting? It might help you relax a little."

"I can't relax," she said, smoothing her hands over the skirt of her dress. "As soon as they get here, I have to drop the pasta in the pot of water boiling on the stove."

"Eager to feed them and rush them out the door again?" he teased.

"That and I'm worried the eggplant will end up overcooked and soggy again," she said.

He poured the glass of wine anyway and pressed it into her hand.

"I'm being ridiculous, aren't I?" She lifted the glass to her lips and sipped.

"I wouldn't say you're being ridiculous," he denied. "But you do seem a little uptight."

"I don't have the best relationship with my sister," she reminded him.

"And what's your relationship with your ex?"

She shrugged. "We're friends."

"That's all?" he pressed. "The flames of your first love aren't still burning deep inside?"

Erin laughed. "No, I can promise you that any flames, if they ever existed, were completely extinguished a lot of years ago."

"You're one hundred percent completely over him?" he asked, wanting to be sure.

Needing *her* to be sure.

"One hundred percent," she confirmed, nodding.

"Good," he said.

Then he kissed her.

Erin jolted when Kyle's lips brushed over hers.

And again, half a second later, when a knock sounded on the door.

She'd barely had a chance to register the fact that *Kyle was kissing her* before he was drawing away again. And as she exhaled an unsteady breath, she silently cursed her sister's lousy timing.

But maybe she should be grateful for the interruption, because kissing Kyle was…

Her emotions were in such a tangle, she honestly had no idea how to finish that thought.

Kissing Kyle was…

A surprise.

A long-harbored fantasy finally realized.

A definite pleasure.

And the fleeting touch of his lips made her want more.

A lot more.

Again, her mind filled with possibilities: *What if*…

But she didn't have time to sort through those possibilities now. And even if she did, she didn't think she was capable of doing so while her head was still spinning from the effects of that all-too-brief, never-should-have-happened kiss.

A second—and louder—knock sounded.

"You should get that," Kyle said.

She nodded. "Can you dump the spaghetti in the pot?"

"Don't you think you should open the door first— to make sure it's actually Anna and Nick?"

"Okay. Sure. Right."

The corners of his mouth tipped up, just a little, in response to her apparent befuddlement, proving that she was the only one affected by their kiss.

She started to turn away.

Kyle, realizing that she still had her wineglass in hand, carefully plucked it from Erin's grasp.

She pasted a smile on her face and opened the door to welcome her sister and brother-in-law.

"It's good to see you," Erin said, surprised to realize it was true as she hugged her sister. "Congratulations."

Anna fairly glowed with happiness. "Thank you."

She hugged Nick next and offered her best wishes to him, too. "I'm so happy for both of you."

"Are you really?" her sister asked, sounding worried.

"Of course, I am," she assured her.

Anna smiled, visibly relieved. "We were a little worried that you might not approve of our marriage."

Obviously not worried enough to talk to her sister before the exchange of vows, but Erin pushed that thought aside.

"Anna was worried," Nick clarified with a wink. "I tried to assure her that you'd tossed me back like an undersized trout a long time ago."

An analogy that wasn't nearly as charming as he probably thought, Erin mused.

"As long as you're happy, I'm happy," she said, ushering her guests into the apartment.

"Oh." Anna halted in her tracks. *"Wow."*

Erin followed her sister's gaze to see what had snagged her attention—and found her gaze fixed on the man in the kitchen.

"Major hot guy alert," Anna said.

Her husband cleared his throat.

"Not as hot as you, of course," she hastily replied.

"Of course," he echoed dryly.

Thankfully, Kyle couldn't hear the exchange over the hum of the fan over the stove.

"Please, come in and make yourselves comfortable," Erin said. "Can I get you something to drink? Beer? Wine? Soda?"

"Water for me, please," Anna said.

"I'll have a Coke," Nick said.

She retreated to the kitchen, where Kyle was filling a glass with water from the dispenser in the door of the fridge. A can of Coke was already on the counter.

"Apparently you *can* hear over the hum of the fan," she noted.

He just grinned.

Before delivering the drinks to her guests, she grabbed her wineglass and swallowed a mouthful of cabernet sauvignon.

"Is the pasta on?" she asked Kyle.

"The water just came back to a boil," he said. "Go ahead and drop it in."

"You're determined to make me make dinner, aren't you?"

"You did make dinner," he said, as she set down her wine and slid the premeasured spaghetti into the water. "And you should be proud of what you've cooked."

"Thank you," she said sincerely. "For everything, but especially for being here right now."

"My pleasure."

She gave the pasta a minute to soften before stirring to ensure the strands didn't clump. Then she put down the spoon and picked up the drinks he'd readied. "And now it's time to introduce you to the bride and groom."

Kyle followed her to the living room, then shook hands with and offered his congratulations to the happy couple.

"We felt just a little bit guilty about eloping," Anna confided. "So we sprang for the deluxe wedding package, including a video of our vows. Do you want to see it?"

"Oh. Um." Erin glanced at her watch. "Actually, dinner's going to be ready in less than ten minutes."

"Could we eat a little bit later?" her sister asked hopefully. "I'm not really very hungry right now."

"We were late stopping for lunch," Nick explained.

"My fault," his bride confessed, not sounding the least bit apologetic. "I desperately wanted to try an In-N-Out burger and wouldn't settle for anything else."

"I didn't realize In-N-Out did a veggie burger," Erin said.

Nick snorted. "She didn't have a veggie burger. She had a double cheeseburger."

Anna elbowed him in the ribs. "It had lettuce and tomato on it!"

"You're right," he said, placatingly.

"But…you told me that you're a vegetarian," Erin said.

"I am." A slow smile curved Anna's lips. "But the baby wanted meat."

Chapter Four

*B*aby.

Erin shouldn't have been surprised. Hadn't both Kyle and Lucy suspected that a pregnancy was responsible for the hasty wedding? But she'd preferred to believe that Anna and Nick were simply head over heels in love. After all, she'd seen evidence of their mutual affection when she was in Silver Hook for Christmas.

Still, deep down, she'd suspected that her friends might be right. And once the initial shock of her sister's announcement had passed, she felt a spurt of joy to realize that she was going to be an aunt…again.

Of course, that was immediately followed by a twinge of concern that Anna might have felt forced into a marriage she wasn't ready for because she was pregnant—and then a teensy stab of envy that her little sister was soon going to have the family that Erin herself had always, albeit secretly, coveted.

"So you are pregnant," she murmured aloud.

"Why else would we be in such a hurry to get married?" Anna asked.

"Congratulations," Kyle said, when Erin remained silent. "Again."

Anna beamed at the chef. "Thank you."

Erin finally recovered her voice. "Well, let's see this wedding video," she suggested.

"Yay!" Her sister clapped her hands.

"While you get it set up, we'll check on dinner," Kyle said, grabbing Erin's arm and steering her back to the kitchen.

Once out of view of her guests, she leaned back against the counter and let out a long, slow breath.

"You okay?" he asked.

She nodded. "Yeah. It's just…a lot. My little sister isn't just married, she's going to have a baby."

He lifted the pot of pasta off the stove and dumped the spaghetti into the strainer. "I hate to state the obvious, but your little sister is all grown up."

"I know."

"And having a baby with your ex."

"I heard that, too," she said.

"I just wondered if that might be the real reason your head is spinning," he said.

"I told you before that I got over Nick a long time ago."

Before her sister and brother-in-law arrived.

Before Kyle kissed her.

"You did," he confirmed. "But I didn't know if seeing him again might have stirred up any old feelings."

She shook her head. "It didn't."

"Good to know," he said, pulling open the drawer under her stove to retrieve a frying pan.

Why was it good to know?

Because he might want to kiss her again?

She certainly hoped he would, and that was the real reason her head was spinning.

Anna's announcement would have thrown her for a loop anyway, but coming as it did so soon after Kyle's kiss, was it any wonder Erin was feeling as if the ground was unsteady beneath her feet?

He, on the other hand, didn't seem affected at all, she noted, watching as he moved around the kitchen. Of course, if his reputation was to be believed, he'd kissed so many women that the brief touch of their lips probably hadn't even registered in his mind— and if she was smart, she'd push it firmly out of hers, too.

"What are you doing to do with that?" she asked curiously, as he found the olive oil in the cupboard beside the stove and drizzled some in the pan.

"We'll use it to reheat the pasta when we're ready to eat."

"You mean I don't have to start over again with fresh pasta?"

He gave her a look that she couldn't quite decipher. "No."

"That's a relief," she said. "Because I'm pretty sure that was my last box of spaghetti."

"Everything's going to work out just fine."

"Are you referring to dinner? Or something else?"

He grinned. "Let's go watch a wedding."

"Did you hear what Anna said?" Her sister and brother-in-law's car had barely pulled away when Erin turned to him, her hands on her hips.

"You're going to have to be more specific," Kyle said cautiously. "Your sister didn't stop talking the whole time she was here."

"The part where she said that she had a cheeseburger for lunch," she clarified. "A *double* cheeseburger."

He nodded. "I heard."

"That's *two* meat patties."

"It is," he agreed.

"I had the chicken parm nailed." She paced across the floor. "Okay, it took me a few tries, but I did it— and then I had to start from scratch again because she told me she didn't eat meat."

"For what it's worth, I think you nailed the eggplant parm, too," he said.

"I've never been a fan of eggplant," she confided. "Truth be told, I'm not a big fan of Anna right now, either."

"Sibling relationships can be challenging," he acknowledged.

"How would you know? You and Lucy have a great relationship."

"Now," he acknowledged. "But we had our fair share of battles over the years. My mom would probably say more than our fair share. Actually, though, I was thinking about my other siblings."

Kyle so rarely talked about his father's other family that Erin sometimes forgot he had two brothers and another sister.

"I guess you do know," she acknowledged.

He refilled her empty wineglass, earning a smile of thanks.

"But how do you always seem to know what I need?" she asked now.

"Because I sat across from you at dinner, and it was exactly what I needed," he said, pouring a second glass for himself.

She took her wine to the living room, where she dropped down onto the sofa and propped her feet up on the coffee table—drawing Kyle's attention to the length of shapely leg stretched out beneath the hem of her short skirt.

"Despite the whole dinner fiasco, I'm glad they stopped by," she said now. "And that I got to see the video of their wedding. It was a beautiful ceremony, wasn't it?"

"Sure," he agreed. "Though I'm not sure a Vegas wedding is legal if it's not officiated by Elvis."

She smiled again. "Well, legal or not, I hope they have a long and happy life together."

He hoped so, too, but he didn't think the newlyweds were as head over heels in love as they were pretending to be. Because while Erin was watching the video of the bride and groom exchanging vows, Kyle had been watching the bride and groom.

Erin was adamant that any feelings she had for Nick Burnett were long gone, but Kyle had picked up a different vibe from her ex that made him suspect their romantic history wasn't as firmly in the past for him. And the way Anna had clung to her husband, constantly touching him to draw his attention back to her, the man's bride knew it, too.

Throughout the course of their friendship, Kyle had heard a lot of Erin's family stories, so he knew that Anna wasn't just the youngest of four children but her mother's obvious favorite. He might have wanted to dispute the claim, but Erin had said it in such a matter-of-fact tone, without resentment or blame, that he'd realized even if it wasn't true, she believed it to be so.

"My mom almost died giving birth to me," she'd explained to him a long time ago. *"But with Anna, she barely broke a sweat during labor.*

"'The most perfect childbirth experience ever,' she always said. 'Resulting in the most perfect baby.'

"Not just perfect but beautiful," Erin confided. *"With pretty blond curls and big blue eyes."*

In fact, she'd been such a beautiful baby that Bonnie Napper had entered her youngest daughter in a local beauty pageant for infants and toddlers, leading to Anna being named "Cutest Little Hooker" three years in a row.

Kyle had choked on his drink when Erin told him that, certain she must be joking. But apparently the brilliant minds behind the pageant in Silver Hook saw nothing wrong with the title.

To his way of thinking, Erin would have been well within her rights to resent Anna, but he got the impression—not just from everything she'd ever told him but also from what he'd observed during tonight's visit—that she adored her little sister as much as everyone else in the family did.

Sitting close to both sisters at dinner, he'd noticed that there was a definite resemblance between them in that they both had blond hair and blue eyes. But Erin's hair was thicker and shinier, her eyes darker and bluer. It was as if Anna was a less vibrant copy of her older sibling, and judging by the way she kept pushing herself into the center of the conversation, she was well aware of it.

To her credit, though, she seemed sincerely devoted to her husband. And while he suspected that she could have set her sights higher than Nick Burnett, it was a bigger surprise to Kyle to meet the man who'd once won Erin's heart. The outdoorsman was tall and skinny, with thick-framed glasses and spiky hair that had probably been a popular style when he was in high school—which was, of course, when he'd actually dated Erin.

"I just hope they're ready to be parents," she said now. "Anna's barely twenty-eight and Nick acts even younger."

"If they're not ready now, they've got almost seven months to get ready," Kyle pointed out.

"I know Nick's always dreamed of having a big

family, but I can't recall Anna ever mentioning wanting kids. Then again, I'm probably not the one she'd confide in. We don't talk about things like that," Erin admitted. "I've certainly never told her that, as much as I sometimes think I want to be a mom, I'm afraid I'll replicate the relationship I have with mine."

"I know you and your mother aren't exactly close," he acknowledged, "but why would you think that would affect your relationship with your own child?"

"I always assumed it was the physical trauma of childbirth that prevented her from connecting with me. But what if there's some kind of maternal gene that helps a new mom bond with her baby…and what if I don't have it?"

"Not that I've given it much thought in anything more than a vague sure-I'd-like-to-be-a-mom-someday kind of way," she continued, without giving him a chance to respond to her question. "But maybe that's because I haven't had sex in forever and a real relationship in a lot longer than that."

He should circle back to her concerns about motherhood and offer some kind of reassurance, but the last part of her remark seemed much more relevant in the here and now.

"How long is forever?" he asked, his curiosity piqued.

She shook her head, her cheeks turning pink. "I didn't mean to say that part out loud."

He grinned. "But since you did…how long is forever?"

She ignored the question. "The problem is that

you're so easy to talk to, I sometimes forget to filter what I say."

"That's not a problem. We're friends. You
shouldn't have to filter what you say to me."

"And tonight was a reminder of only some of the
many reasons I'm glad we're friends," she said. "I
can't thank you enough for being here."

"Because I rescued the pasta?" he guessed.

"Your impressive culinary skills are the least of
it," she said. "You also knew I was on edge before
Anna and Nick got here and you managed to distract me."

"How did I do that?"

She sipped her wine. "You're going to make me
say it, aren't you?"

"If you don't say it, how am I supposed to know
what you're talking about?" he pointed out reason-
ably.

"Fine, I'll say it," she decided. "Because not talking about it hasn't stopped me thinking about it."

He waited.

But she took another sip of wine before she said,
"I'm talking about the kiss."

He shifted on the sofa then so that he was facing
her. "The barely-a-kiss that was interrupted by the
untimely arrival of the newlyweds?"

She gave a jerky nod.

"You think that was intended as a distraction?"

She stared at the burgundy liquid in her glass. "I
can't think of any other reason that you'd kiss me."

"How about the fact that you're smart and beautiful and, after more than six years, I finally decided to stop ignoring the attraction that's been simmering between us since the beginning?"

Erin swallowed another mouthful of wine to moisten her suddenly dry throat.

"I guess that could be an alternative explanation," she finally acknowledged.

"It's the truth," he said.

"Now I wish Anna and Nick had shown up at least thirty seconds later."

"Why thirty seconds?" he asked.

She shrugged. "I figure that's how long it would take for me to know how it feels to really be kissed by you."

His lips curved. "It would take a lot longer than that."

The words sounded like more than a statement of fact—they sounded like a promise. And everything inside Erin quivered with anticipation, ignoring the warning of her brain that they were edging toward dangerous territory.

She lowered her feet to the ground and set her wineglass on the coffee table, then sidled closer to him. "Show me."

Kyle dipped his head, and anticipation caused Erin's breath to back up in her lungs as butterflies took flight in her belly. But instead of finding her mouth, his lips brushed over the curve of her cheek, then skimmed her jaw below her ear, making her shiver. His touch was gentle, more of a caress than a kiss, and unbelievably arousing.

"You're supposed to be kissing me," she said, feeling breathless already.

"I am," he told her, as his lips continued to graze her skin.

Hers parted on a sigh of pleasure when he finally captured them with his own. His mouth was warm and firm, with just the right amount of pressure. And when his tongue touched the seam of her lips, she welcomed the deepening of the kiss.

He was right. Thirty seconds wasn't nearly long enough to experience the pleasure of being kissed by Kyle Landry. But as their tongues dallied and danced together, time lost all meaning for Erin. She didn't know how long the kiss went on, she only knew that she never wanted it to end.

He continued to kiss her as he drew her onto his lap, so that she was straddling his hips with her knees, her skirt up around her thighs. His oh-so-skillful hands moved over her, sliding up her back, down her arms, making her shiver. Making her yearn.

She pressed closer to him, relishing the heat and hardness of his body against hers, reveling in the sensual assault of his mouth on hers.

Who knew that he could kiss like this?

Certainly not Erin, because if she'd known, there was no way she would have resisted her feelings for him for six years.

Or maybe she would have, because they were *friends*.

And a surefire way to ruin their friendship would

be to give in to the attraction between them. He was right about that, too. The attraction had been there all along, simmering beneath the surface, leading inexorably to this moment.

She remembered the first time she'd ever met him, five days before Lucy and Claudio's wedding. The bride had sent her brother to pick up her maid of honor from the airport in Elko, and when Erin had turned away from the luggage carousel and her eyes had met Kyle's, she'd felt the reverberations right down to her toes. Of course, that was before she'd known who he was. Because while the idea of a holiday romance was momentarily intriguing—especially to a woman who hadn't been naked with a guy for longer than she could remember—she knew it was a Very Bad Idea to hook up with her best friend's brother.

As soon as Kyle introduced himself, Erin realized that she should have recognized him from the numerous photos her roommate had shown her over the years. But those photos hadn't done him justice—and they certainly hadn't prepared her for meeting the man in the flesh.

And she was admittedly disappointed to know that nothing could ever happen between them, because something could only lead to all kinds of awkward the morning after. Instead, she ignored the tingle that skated through her veins when he shook her hand, the tremble that weakened her knees when he smiled at her and even the tug of longing that pulled in her belly every time she breathed in his scent on the forty-five-minute drive from Elko to Haven.

Because he was off-limits.

Her best friend's brother.

Over the next few days, she'd spent a fair amount of time with him as they helped with preparations for the wedding. During that time, she discovered that he wasn't just incredibly handsome but charming and funny—and an amazingly talented chef who chafed at the restrictions imposed upon him by his boss at Jo's Pizza, who also happened to be his mom.

Having some mother issues of her own, Erin had empathized with him over a sausage and roasted red pepper pizza. While they were chatting, Quinn Ellison had come in to pick up her order and commented to Kyle that the pizzeria's revamped website had forced her to admit that she needed to update her own. Kyle was happy to introduce the local suspense writer to the creative talent behind the vision, which ultimately led to Quinn hiring Erin to redesign and maintain her website. And in the years since, the bestselling author had become not just her biggest client but one of her best friends.

Erin would always be grateful to Kyle for helping her make that connection, which was yet one more reason she'd felt the need to ignore the hum of attraction whenever she was with him. It didn't seem right to repay his helpfulness by making a move on him. Especially when he'd given no indication that he might welcome such a move.

So she'd buried her feelings deep, but recently, they'd started to push their way to the surface again.

She hadn't noticed—or maybe she hadn't let herself hope—that he was attracted to her, too. But the way he was kissing her right now definitely held promise.

After what seemed like only minutes but might have been forever, he finally eased his mouth from hers, his breathing as labored as her own.

"I should probably head over to the restaurant," he said, when he managed to speak.

But his arms were still around her, as if he was reluctant to let her go.

And she didn't want to be let go.

Not yet.

Not when there was still so much new and interesting to explore between them.

"No." Erin shook her head. "You should stay."

Chapter Five

Kyle held her gaze for a long minute. "Are you sure?"

Erin didn't hesitate to respond: "I'm sure."

His lips curved slowly. "Bedroom?"

She knew he was asking permission rather than directions, and she nodded.

He lifted her with him as he rose to his feet. She hooked her legs around his waist and linked her arms around his neck, holding on to him as he made his way down the hall. He paused inside the doorway of her bedroom and lowered her feet to the ground, then dipped his head and kissed her again.

She sighed in blissful pleasure as his tongue slid between her lips, and shivered as his hands moved over her body, his palms caressing her skin through the silky fabric of her dress, stoking her desire. But she wanted to touch him, too. She wanted to feel the press of his naked body against hers, inside hers. She opened the button and unzipped his jeans, then reached inside his boxer briefs to wrap her fingers around his hard, velvety length.

With their mouths still fused together, she felt as much as heard him groan as she stroked him. Once… twice…before he captured her wrist and gently removed her hand.

"We've waited too long to rush this now," he told her.

"We've waited too long," she agreed. "I don't want to wait another minute."

He tipped his forehead to rest against hers. "I'm trying to show some restraint here."

"I don't want restraint. I want to know that you want me as much as I want you."

"I do," he promised, and whisked the dress over her head before dispensing with his own clothes and lowering her onto the bed, covering her naked body with his own.

She trembled, more eager than nervous, as his weight pressed her into the mattress. She knew he worked out—he often joked that he needed to hit the gym to compensate for the number of calories he consumed in the kitchen, sampling this and that. Still, she hadn't expected his muscles to be so sculpted, his skin so taut. Her hands moved over his body, a truly pleasurable exploration and discovery.

"Do you have a condom handy or should I dig

my wallet out of the pocket of my pants—which are somewhere on the floor?" he asked.

"I've got one," she said, reaching for the drawer of her night table, then hesitating.

"Please tell me you're not having second thoughts now," he said.

"No second thoughts," she promised. "I'm just trying to remember when I bought the box of condoms shoved way in the back of this drawer."

"Considering that you haven't had sex in *forever*," he said, quoting her. "It was probably a long time ago."

She pulled out a square packet and held it close to her face, looking for a date imprinted on the wrapper and breathing a sigh of relief when she found it—and confirmed that it wasn't outdated.

"We're good," she said, offering him the square packet.

He carefully tore open the wrapper and sheathed himself.

"Tell me again that you're sure," he said, brushing his lips over hers.

"I'm so sure that if you're not inside me in the next thirty seconds, I'm going to scream," she told him.

"I'm hoping that you'll scream when I *am* inside you."

She couldn't believe he was teasing her at a time like this—but even as she felt her cheeks flush with heat, she countered with "Make me."

He nibbled playfully on her bottom lip. "You know I can't resist a challenge."

"I do know," she admitted, as his mouth moved over her jaw, down her throat, trailing kisses along the way. His hands were just as busy as his mouth, exploring her curves and contours, touching and teasing until she was quivering all over. Her heart was pounding; her blood was pulsing; her body was yearning.

"Kyle. Please."

He nudged her legs apart, and her breath quickened in anticipation of his hard length inside her. Filling and fulfilling her. Then anticipation became reality, and it was So. Much. Better. than she'd imagined.

His movements were deliberate. Slow, deep strokes that seemed to touch her very center, pushing her closer and closer to the edge…and finally…over.

She cried out as the first wave of the climax washed over her, proof that he'd met her challenge. And his lips were curved in a smug smile as they captured hers again, swallowing her sounds of ecstasy as wave after wave of pleasure crashed over her and swept her away.

It was dark when Kyle awakened, with Erin's naked body snuggled close to his. They'd made love two more times during the night, and yet arousal stirred in him again. It took every ounce of willpower he possessed to inch away from her and ease out from under the covers when what he really wanted to do was roll her onto her back and join their bodies together again.

Though it was early still—too early for most people—he had places to go. The local farmers would soon be stocking their market shelves with fresh produce, and he was always one of the first customers, as happy as a kid in a candy store to explore the various offerings and imagine how he might incorporate them into his menu at the restaurant.

Erin didn't stir as he dressed, quickly and quietly, in the dark, and he breathed a sigh of relief as he slipped out of her apartment. They were going to have to talk about what had happened the night before, there was no way around it. But while he had no regrets about making love with her, he was admittedly a little apprehensive about that chat.

He didn't think she would expect—or even want—one night of lovemaking to miraculously transform their friendship into a romance. But getting naked with a woman—even one who was a longtime friend—had a way of changing a relationship, and it would be foolish to pretend otherwise.

Thankfully, Erin knew that he wasn't looking for any kind of long-term commitments. She understood that he had no intention of ever marrying or having a family—no way was he going to risk turning out like his dad, who'd abandoned his first wife and kids, or his mom, who'd prioritized her restaurant over all else. But in order to resume the status quo, they needed to remember that they'd been friends first, and that neither of them wanted to risk that friendship by pretending it could lead to something more.

Which meant that there could be no repeat of what had happened between them last night.

Because friends-with-benefits might sound like a good idea, but he'd been down that road before and inevitably one of the friends wanted more, and then even the friendship was lost. He couldn't risk that happening with Erin. Not only because he valued her friendship too much but also because she was his sister's best friend.

He winced, imagining how Lucy might react if she knew that he'd spent the night in Erin's bed. His sister would undoubtedly be furious with him. She probably wouldn't be too happy with Erin, either, but she'd blame Kyle. Because she'd warned him, years ago when she'd sent him to the airport to pick up her friend, that Erin was off-limits.

At the time, he'd laughed at her fierce warning and promised that he had no interest in hooking up with her college pal. Then Erin had walked off the plane and he'd cursed himself for offering an assurance he wasn't sure he could keep.

Erin breathed a sigh of relief when she woke up and discovered that Kyle was gone. She didn't think he'd snuck out to avoid an awkward "morning after" conversation. She knew that Thursday was a market day, and Kyle liked to be there early to get his pick of the crop. She'd gone with him once, and she'd actually enjoyed the sights and scents of the market— though not enough to want to get up with the sun on a regular basis.

His absence now meant that she'd have some time to figure out what to say before she saw him again. Because they were definitely going to have to talk about what had happened between them the night before—and where they would go from here.

She stepped under the spray of the shower, wincing as she soaped up her limbs and felt little tugs in muscles that hadn't had a workout in far too long—and had been very thoroughly worked out the night before. She hadn't been surprised to discover that Kyle was every bit as talented and creative in the bedroom as he was in the kitchen, and she was admittedly disappointed to know that there wouldn't be a repeat performance. Because as amazing as their lovemaking had been, there was no way she could allow it to happen again.

She had no regrets about their night together, but she also had no interest in a friends-with-benefits arrangement. Mostly because she'd never been particularly good at sharing her body without opening her heart, and she knew that if she made the mistake of falling in love with Kyle, she'd end up with it in pieces. He would never hurt her on purpose—he didn't ever intend to hurt any of the women whose hearts he'd trampled in the past—but the lack of intent wouldn't mitigate the result.

He'd told her more than once that serious relationships weren't for him. *I enjoy the company of beautiful women, but cooking is my passion and the restaurant is my priority. And I'm always up-front*

*about that fact when I start dating a woman—so why
do they expect it to change?*

Erin hadn't been able to answer his question then,
and she wasn't going to make the mistake of becom-
ing one of those women now simply because they'd
spent the night together.

In addition to worrying about how she could re-
store the status quo with Kyle, she was also worried
about her relationship with his sister. Because there
was no way she could keep a secret like this from
her, and she had no idea how Lucy would respond to
the discovery that her best friend had gotten naked
with her brother.

She was concerned that Lucy might be upset, but
her bigger concern was that she might try to roman-
ticize the situation. Since she'd fallen in love with
and married Claudio, Lucy had been eager for Erin to
follow the same path, even going so far as to imagine
that they'd have kids close in age so they could grow
up together. And while Erin wasn't completely op-
posed to the idea of getting married and maybe having a family of her own someday, she knew it wasn't
going to happen with her friend's brother.

Kyle had made it clear to Erin—and to every
woman he'd ever dated—that he had no interest in
marriage or kids. Not that this information had dissuaded many of his girlfriends, more than one of
whom had been certain she'd be the one to change
his mind. But Erin knew his family history, and she
understood that his determination to remain single
was about more than loving the bachelor life—it was

about feeling abandoned by the father who'd walked out on his family when Kyle was only ten years old and neglected by the mother who'd spent most of her waking hours at the restaurant. So she definitely wasn't going to ruin their friendship by trying to turn it into something more just because they'd shared one night of off-the-charts lovemaking.

When Erin didn't immediately answer his knock, Kyle suspected that she was probably in the shower and decided to use his emergency key—the same one he'd used to lock up when he left her apartment only a few hours earlier—to let himself in. He didn't hear the water running, which immediately obliterated his wayward fantasy of stripping down and joining her.

And that was a good thing, he reminded himself. Because while he hadn't been able to prevent his mind wandering down that tantalizing path, he'd already decided that they couldn't go there again. And maybe, if he kept reminding himself of that fact, his brain would eventually transmit the message to his ready and willing body.

"Erin?"

The only response was a sniffle from somewhere down the hall.

He paused in mid-step.

Was she…crying?

There it was again.

Another sniffle.

Damn, she was crying.

Was it his fault? Was she upset because he'd left

without saying goodbye? Should he have left a note on the bedside table?

Should he leave now?

Emotions usually made him uncomfortable, but Erin wasn't quick to tears, which meant that there was no way he could turn away from her now.

A few more steps down the hall and he was standing in the doorway of her bedroom. The sheets they'd tangled up the night before had been untangled and the bed was now neatly made. But it was the suitcase open on top of the bed that made his heart drop.

"What are you doing?"

Erin jolted at the sound of his voice, obviously so deep in her own thoughts that she hadn't heard him come in or call out to her.

"I'm packing," she said, stating the obvious.

"But…why?"

"I have to go home." She continued to pull clothes out of her dresser and toss them into the suitcase. "My mom called…my dad's sick."

"Sick?" he echoed, uncomprehending.

"He had a doctor's appointment this morning. It was just supposed to be a routine follow-up to some tests." She continued to pack as she talked. "At least that's what they thought." She drew in a deep breath, let it out on a shudder. "Until the doctor said he has stage four colon cancer."

He didn't know exactly what that meant, but he knew that stage four any kind of cancer was bad.

"He has an appointment with the oncologist on

Monday." She closed the lid of the suitcase and zipped it shut. "I need to be there."

"Of course," he agreed.

"I don't know how long I'm going to be gone. It might be a few weeks. Maybe longer."

"Will you keep me posted?" he asked.

She nodded. "But you're probably going to need to hire someone else, for the interim."

"I'm not worried about the restaurant—I'm worried about *you*."

"I'm okay." Erin managed a weak smile. "I have to be, because my mom is completely falling apart, and somebody has to hold it together. Of course, she hasn't reached out to my sister yet, because she doesn't want to upset Anna while she's on her honeymoon—even if that honeymoon is only a string of Dusty Boots Motels between Las Vegas and Silver Hook."

But it was okay to upset Erin, because her mom knew that she'd drop everything to rush back home.

"Do you want me to take you to the airport?"

"No, thanks. I couldn't get a flight out before tomorrow afternoon, and since it will be convenient to have a vehicle when I'm there, I decided to drive."

"You're going to *drive* to Arkansas?"

"I've done it before," she told him.

He knew that she had, and though he'd always worried about her making the long journey alone, he'd trusted that she could take care of herself. And if he said anything to object to her plans now, she might think he was being overprotective—like a boyfriend rather than just a friend—because they'd spent the night together.

"But not when you're obviously upset and worried," he pointed out gently. "Maybe you should wait and—"

"No." She grabbed another suitcase and began filling it as haphazardly as she'd done the first. "I don't want to wait."

"Then let me take you."

"It's a sixteen-hundred-mile trip," she reminded him. "There's no way you can drive me home and be back in time for dinner prep."

Obviously not, but he wasn't going to let that detail dissuade him. "Giselle can cover for a few days."

"Giselle already covered for you last night."

"She's very capable," he pointed out.

Erin managed a smile. "I know. And I appreciate the offer, really, but I'll be fine."

"Okay," he relented. "But why are you packing up everything you own?"

"I just want to be prepared for all contingencies."

"If you get there and realize that you've forgotten something you want, let me know and I'll ship it to you."

She nodded, her eyes shiny with fresh tears. "Thank you."

"You don't need to thank me," he told her. "I'm here for you, and I'll always be here for you, because we're friends."

Even if, for one night, they'd been more.

Though that night had ended only a few hours

earlier, he imagined that it felt like a lifetime ago to Erin, whose whole world had been turned upside down by a phone call.

And he didn't realize how much he'd miss her until she was gone.

Chapter Six

It was still early enough when Kyle left the farmer's market that he felt confident he'd be able to catch his mom at home. Mondays and Fridays were delivery days at the restaurant, and while any of her staff was capable of handling the receiving, she preferred to be on-site to ensure there weren't any problems. She claimed that the success of Jo's Pizza could be credited to her oversight of even the smallest details. Kyle would argue—and he had—that her micromanagement style prevented her employees from realizing their potential. It was only one of many disagreements they'd had over the years that had ultimately led to his decision to find a job elsewhere.

But today was Thursday, so he knocked on the heavy wooden door of the modest bungalow that she'd bought before his last year of high school. The house was a definite step up from the apartment over the restaurant, but it wasn't far away, and even now, his mom usually walked to work—and home again at the end of a long day.

"This is a surprise," she said, when she opened the door.

Kyle held up a paper bag. "I brought you fresh strawberries from the market."

"Another surprise," she said, stepping away from the door to allow him entry. "I didn't expect to see them for another week or so."

"They're early this year," he confirmed, as he followed her to the kitchen.

She took the quart-size container out of the bag to look them over. "Oh, they are perfectly ripe and beautiful." She drew in a deep breath. "And they smell as good as they look."

He nodded his agreement. "I'm adding a spinach and strawberry salad with candied pecans and feta to the menu tonight."

She wrinkled her nose as she reached into the cupboard for a mug. "People actually order salad with fruit and nuts?"

"People love salad with fruit and nuts," he told her. "Our field greens with pear, walnut and blue cheese is another popular one, as is the arugula salad with grilled peaches, toasted almonds and a honey vinaigrette."

"What's wrong with a traditional garden salad?" she asked, dropping a coffee pod into the Keurig.

She was referring, of course, to the small bowl of romaine lettuce with a few slices of cucumber, a sprinkle of matchstick carrots and a couple of cherry tomatoes with Italian dressing that had been a staple at Jo's for as long as he could remember.

Not even Caesar or Greek salads had ever made it to her menu. "Fads," she'd insisted, when he'd suggested expanding the healthy options they offered.

"Well, thank you for the strawberries," she said. "But I'll eat mine as God intended—on top of shortcake with a mountain of whipped cream."

He smiled at that. "Enjoy. And now I should probably be heading over to the restaurant."

But he made no move to leave, and she offered him the mug of fresh coffee.

"On the other hand, I can probably spare a few more minutes," he said, accepting it.

"You're missing Erin," she guessed.

He lifted a shoulder, feigning a casualness that didn't fool his mother for a minute.

"Have you heard from her recently?"

"A few days ago."

Jo picked up her own half-empty mug and sipped. "How's her dad doing?"

"I don't really know," he admitted. "The prognosis doesn't seem great, but every time we talk, she sounds so relentlessly upbeat."

His mother nodded, understanding. "Because she doesn't want to admit that he might be dying."

It was a possibility that Kyle didn't want to consider, either. And one that had got him thinking about his own father—and wondering if he should make an effort to build a relationship with him before it was too late.

Not that Marty Thomas had any health issues that Kyle was aware of, but Brian Napper's diagnosis had been a reminder that bad news could come out of the blue. A truth his mom had learned when both her parents died, suddenly and unexpectedly, in a car crash only a few months after she had separated from her husband.

"Lucy told me that Erin's thinking about subletting her apartment," she said now, drawing his attention back to the present.

He nodded. "Shawna, the night manager at The Stagecoach Inn, was looking for a place for a few months until her new condo is ready."

"Which suggests that Erin's going to be in Arkansas for at least a few months," Jo noted.

"Yeah." And he understood that she'd want to spend as much time as possible with her dad, but she'd been gone only a few weeks and he already wanted her to come home. He'd been surprised to realize how many times he thought about her throughout the day, and how much he missed being able to stop by her apartment just to say hi.

"You should think about taking a few days and going to Silver Hook," his mom suggested.

"I have thought about it," he said, surprising himself as much as her with the admission. "But it's a busy time at the resort and I wouldn't want to be a distraction."

"She might need a distraction. And I have no doubt she could use a friend."

"Maybe Quinn can take a trip," he suggested as an alternative. "She always says that, as long as she's got her laptop, she can work anywhere. My job doesn't offer the same flexibility."

"Is it the job that's inflexible—or is it you?" his mom wondered aloud.

Kyle bristled. "What's that supposed to mean?"

"It means that you don't have a life outside of the restaurant."

"I can't believe *you*, of all people, would say that to me," he said, feeling not just defensive but annoyed. "All I'm doing is following in your footsteps."

"The difference between us is that I didn't have any choice but to pour every ounce of energy into the restaurant."

"Every single day, from midmorning until late at night."

"Someone had to make the pizza."

"You could have hired someone to help out," he pointed out. "So that you could spend a couple of nights a week with your kids."

"Is that what you think? That I chose to be at the restaurant rather than spend time with my family?"

Of course, it was what he'd thought, because he'd been a kid who didn't understand why she was never around. But seeing the stricken expression on his mother's face now, he was forced to acknowledge that his assumptions might have been wrong.

"You have no idea." She shook her head. "And

why would you? I didn't want you or Lucy to know how shaky our financial situation was.

"But the truth is, in those early days, I was barely able to pay a server and a dishwasher to work Friday and Saturday nights—but on every other night, when the restaurant wasn't so busy, I waited on customers and did the cleanup myself."

Had he blocked out those memories—or simply forgotten all the times that he'd sat at one of the tables covered with a red-and-white-checked cloth, doing his homework while his mom was busy in the kitchen?

But now, as the hurt in her tone struck home, he remembered all that and so much more, such as the time that she'd used the condiment shakers she was refilling to illustrate the answer to a simple math problem—or demonstrated with a pizza how many pieces of an eight-slice pie would be left if five were eaten.

And now that he really stopped to think about it, he was ashamed to discover that he'd never understood nor appreciated how many tasks she'd been juggling—nor given her near enough credit for all that she'd accomplished.

"You know how much work goes into running a kitchen," she said. "You've done everything from creating a recipe to selecting the best ingredients, from chopping and grilling to plating and serving. But you've never had to worry about paying the bills or wonder which vendor might be willing to cut you a little slack if you can't pay the full amount in any given month, because nothing is more important to you than keeping a roof over the heads of your children and food on their table."

"You're right," Kyle said now. "And I'm sorry I never considered how much responsibility you carried as a business owner and single mom."

"I don't want you to be sorry," Jo said gently. "I just want a better life for you. A more balanced life."

"What if I'm happy with my life the way it is?"

"You can be happy and still want more," she told him. "And you deserve more."

He didn't ask her to define "more," because he knew she was thinking that he should want to get married and have a family. But after Marty walked out on his family, Kyle had decided that a wife and kids weren't ever going to be a part of his plan. He wasn't going to take the chance that he might one day follow his father's footsteps out the door.

Erin was exhausted.

Physically, mentally and emotionally exhausted.

She was tired when she went to bed and tired when she woke up, but sleeping in was a luxury she didn't have time for these days.

Sunfish Bay Family Fishing Resort was a family business—it said so right in the name—and the property on the south side of Silver Lake had been in the Napper family for five generations. What was now a resort had originally been nothing more than a three-story lodge and a rickety dock, but over the years, the property had been developed so that there were now a dozen lakefront cabins, a marina and a small general store where guests could buy everything from live bait to travel mugs sporting the Sunfish Bay logo.

Brian Napper was the heart of Sunfish Bay. He'd grown up at the resort, learning everything he needed to know from his father and grandfather. He was part handyman, part mechanic and one hundred percent fisherman. But now he was out of commission, which meant that everyone else had to pick up the slack. Not an easy task in the middle of summer—the height of their busy season.

So Erin stumbled into the kitchen to fill her mug with desperately needed coffee, aware that sleep would have to wait—probably until September.

"There's my favorite girl."

"Ohmygod." She set down her coffee untouched and hurried across the kitchen to hug her brother-in-law. "I didn't know you guys were coming this weekend. When did you get in?"

"It was a last-minute decision," Roger said, folding her in his embrace. "And late last night."

"It's *so* good to see you," she said sincerely.

Though she'd often felt like a fish out of water around her family, she'd never felt that way with her brother's partner. From their very first meeting, Erin had known that Roger was perfect for Owen—and that he would be a wonderful friend and ally to her.

"Family making you crazy?" he guessed.

"Always." She reached into the cupboard for another mug, then filled it full of coffee for him.

"And yet you're here," he noted.

She shrugged. "How could I be anywhere else?"

He nodded his understanding.

"Is Owen still sleeping?"

"Are you kidding? He and Ian were out on the water with your dad before six."

She managed a smile. "Dad will be in his glory."

"He promised there would be fish for dinner," Roger said.

"It's Friday," she pointed out. "We always have fish on Friday."

"I'm already looking forward to it." He sipped his coffee, then asked cautiously, "You're not cooking, are you?"

She narrowed her gaze. "For your information, I'm not quite as inept in the kitchen as everyone wants to believe. In fact, Dad loved the chicken parm that I made last week.

"But no, I'm not cooking. I get to strap on an apron and serve the guests, because Mom thinks that's all I'm good at."

"You are good with customers," he said, his tone placating. "That's probably why you earn the big tips at that fancy restaurant in Haven."

"Well, tomorrow I get to be good at sweeping floors and scrubbing toilets."

"Full turnover this week?"

She nodded. "And we're booked solid through to Labor Day, then most weekends up to Thanksgiving."

"That might explain the bags under your eyes that wouldn't fit in the overhead bin on a 747."

"It's early," she reminded him. "I haven't had a chance to put any makeup on."

"You don't need makeup—you need about twelve hours of uninterrupted sleep."

"Probably," she agreed.

"And a hearty meal," he decided. "How much weight have you lost since you've been home?"

"A few pounds," she guessed. She hadn't actually stepped on a scale in recent weeks, but there was no denying that her clothes were fitting a little looser than usual. "That's what happens when you do manual labor rather than sit on your butt all day."

"Are you sure that's all it is?" he pressed.

"Well, I can't deny that I'm worried about Dad, too." So much so that she didn't feel much like eating half the time, and food didn't sit easily on her tummy when she did.

"We're all worried about Dad," Roger said.

"I didn't figure you guys made the trip from Portland because Owen suddenly had the urge to go fishing."

"It's hard for him, being so far away with all this going on," Roger confided. "Work keeps him busy during the day, and I do the best I can to keep his mind off things at night."

Erin held up a hand. "I don't need those details."

Her brother-in-law grinned. "I wasn't offering to share." Then his expression turned serious. "He's worried that there might not be many weekends left when your dad will be able to go out on the boat."

She sighed. "The chemo is taking its toll on him."

"I've heard that the treatment is sometimes worse than the disease."

"It certainly seems that way. And the worst part? His recent test results indicate that the treatments aren't having any positive effect.

"No," she decided. "The worst part is that he keeps telling me to go back to Haven, to live my own life. But how can I live my life when he might be…" She shook her head, unable to finish the thought, to say the words. "Why doesn't he understand that I need to be here, with him?"

"Because he knows how hard you've worked to establish your career," Roger pointed out. "And he wants to be sure you're not giving it up now to take care of him."

"I'm not giving it up," she promised.

"But are you managing to keep up with your clients?"

"You saw these," she said, pointing to the dark circles under her eyes. "Late at night, after everyone else is settled down to sleep, I open up my laptop and get started."

"You can't keep burning the candle at both ends," her brother-in-law warned.

"You sound just like Lucy," she said.

"So you're keeping in touch with your friends from Haven?"

She nodded. "I FaceTime with her at least once a week, Quinn a little less frequently than that, and Kyle and I exchange a lot of text messages."

"Kyle?" His brows lifted. "Did you have a hookup you didn't tell me about?"

"No," she denied.

Lied.

Roger's next words confirmed that the heat she felt burning her cheeks had revealed the untruth to her all-too-perceptive brother-in-law.

"Did, too," he said, grinning.

"Kyle is Lucy's brother," she told him. "A friend. And kind of my boss."

All completely truthful statements, if not the whole truth.

"Oooh…the hunky chef at The Home Station," Roger realized.

"How do you know he's hunky?"

"We're not just related by marriage, I follow you on Instagram," he reminded her. "And you've posted pictures from the restaurant."

"Anyway," she said, attempting to shift the focus of the conversation. "In answer to your question, yes, I'm keeping in touch with my friends from Haven."

"Uh-uh," he said, shaking his head. "You're not going to distract me so easily."

"I'm not trying to distract you."

He held up two fingers. "That's two lies in less than two minutes," he said, sounding not just disapproving but hurt. "And I didn't think you ever lied to me."

"I don't… Usually."

"So why are you lying to me now?" Roger wondered aloud.

"Because I don't know what to say," she admitted. "Or even how I feel."

"Which tells me that it was more than a hookup," he realized.

"Except that it wasn't," Erin said. "It was just one night."

One incredible, amazing and unforgettable night.

Roger frowned. "Was that your choice or his?"

"Neither, really. Although, if we'd had a chance to talk about it, I'm sure we both would have agreed that it couldn't happen again."

"What do you mean—if you'd had a chance to talk about it?"

"The morning after the night we spent together was when Mom called to tell me about Dad's diagnosis."

"Oh, Erin. I'm so sorry," Roger said.

"The timing wasn't great," she acknowledged.

"But still, you didn't have to drop everything and leave town without talking to the guy about your relationship." He swallowed another mouthful of coffee, his expression contemplative. "Unless you jumped at the opportunity to bail because, as scared as you are for your dad, you're even more scared to have an honest-to-God real relationship."

Erin frowned. "That's ridiculous."

"Is it?" he challenged. "I've been part of this family long enough to have heard the story your grandmother—rest her soul—used to tell at every holiday gathering, about how she had to move back in here after you were born because your mom almost died giving birth to you. According to Grandma Napper, she had to do everything because Bonnie couldn't bear to even hold you for two minutes while her mother-in-law mixed up formula for your bottle."

"Grandma Napper always did like to make every-thing about her," Erin said lightly.

"And she never acknowledged that your mom likely had a severe case of postpartum depression."

"Is there a point to this?"

"The point is that you no doubt heard that story more times than I did over the years, and I worry that you believe it."

"The story's not untrue," she pointed out.

"Just because your mom didn't feed you and change your diapers when you were a baby doesn't mean she doesn't love you."

"I know."

"Do you?" he pressed.

"In my head, I know," she clarified. "But my heart is admittedly a little screwed up."

"So unscrew it," he advised.

"You make it sound so easy."

"Take it from the guy who was engaged to a woman before I met your brother—it's not easy, but it's necessary."

"I'm working on it," she said.

"A task made harder by the fact that you're stuck back here in Silver Hook."

"Only until Dad gets better," she said, desperately needing to believe that he would.

Chapter Seven

Seven weeks after Kyle had watched Erin drive away, she'd yet to give any indication of when she might be coming back to Haven, but her decision to sublet her apartment warned him that it wasn't going to be anytime soon. During that time, they'd remained in fairly regular contact via text messages and occasional phone calls, though he'd twice forgotten about the two-hour time difference between Nevada and Arkansas when he'd called her after closing up the restaurant, wanting to hear her voice just because he'd been thinking about her. Even when he'd woken her up, she'd sounded happy to talk to him—and grateful to talk to about something other than her dad's prognosis and treatment.

Today, he called as he was walking to the restaurant to start the dinner prep.

"I caught you in the middle of something," he realized, when she answered with a breathless hello.

"Cleaning the bathroom," she said.

"Do you want to call me when you're done?"

"No," she said. "I could use a break now. I've been at it for four hours already."

"How dirty is this bathroom?"

She chuckled softly, though her laughter sounded strained. "It's not one bathroom. I'm on cabin cleaning duty today."

"I thought your dad had a treatment today."

"He does. My aunt Mary—my dad's sister—came for a visit, to see how he was doing. And since she offered to take him to his treatment, I volunteered to help Anna with the cleaning. But her pregnancy has made her hypersensitive to certain smells, and even though we use all-natural cleaning products, she had to go for a walk because she was feeling nauseated."

Convenient, Kyle thought, though he didn't dare say so to Erin.

"Lucky for her that you're there to pick up the slack," he said instead.

"Yeah." She sighed. "And there's been a lot of slack. Anytime I ask her to do something, she comes up with some kind of excuse why she can't do it, usually related to her pregnancy. And I feel horrible even saying that, because maybe growing a baby is so incredibly exhausting that she has no energy for anything else."

Despite her claim that she needed a break, he could hear a squeaking sound. Like vinegar on glass. *She's cleaning the mirror. For her sister.*

"Certainly my mom seems to think so," Erin continued. "Because she's always telling Anna to sit down and put her feet up. But even Nick is getting frustrated that she sits round watching cooking shows on TV but doesn't feel inspired to do any actual cooking herself.

"Not that he says anything to her. Or not since the first time, anyway, when she pointed out that it's his fault that she's pregnant. Although, according to Nick, she's the one who assured him that they didn't have to worry about birth control because she was on the Pill—and then she forgot to take it for several days in a row."

Kyle didn't know how to respond to any of that, so he remained silent. On the other end of the line, Erin huffed out a breath.

"Sorry," she said, her tone filled with weariness. "That was too much information, wasn't it?"

"No," he immediately assured her. "You know you can talk to me about anything."

"I do know," she agreed. "But it's not fair to dump all of that on you just because you called."

What wasn't fair, to his mind, was the way everyone dumped their worries and concerns on her. And it frustrated him to know that, in addition to everything she was doing for her mom and dad, her sister's husband—Erin's own ex-boyfriend—was dumping his marital woes on her shoulders—though

Kyle wasn't the least bit surprised to discover that the newlyweds were having some trouble adjusting to married life.

Had Anna honestly forgotten to take her birth control? Or had she purposely not taken it because she wanted to get pregnant? Accidental or deliberate, the fact that Nick was questioning her motives didn't bode well for their marriage.

"You know I'm here for you," he said. "Whatever you need."

"I do know," she agreed. "Talking to you and Lucy and Quinn is the only thing keeping me sane in the midst of all the insanity here.

"But it's not really Anna's fault," she said. "I'm sure it's hard, dealing with all the pregnancy hormones and preparing for the birth of a child while adjusting to being a newlywed."

"She should have thought of that before she trapped her husband into marrying her."

Whoops.

That time he didn't manage to keep the thought inside his head.

"She didn't trap Nick," Erin denied. "Maybe they got married sooner than they'd planned because she was pregnant, but they were already planning to get married."

"Still, she should be careful not to overplay the pregnancy card," he remarked. "Or he's going to resent both her and the baby."

"Do you really think he would?"

He winced at the worry in her tone, because the

last thing he wanted to do was add to the substantial burden she already carried on her slender shoulders.

"I don't know your sister's husband well enough to speak for him," Kyle said. "Maybe he's overjoyed that he's going to be a father. I'm just saying that a lot of guys wouldn't be thrilled to find themselves in that situation."

"Except that Nick loves Anna," Erin said, obviously wanting to believe it was true.

"I'm sure you're right," he agreed, so that she'd have one less concern weighing on her.

"Tell me what's new in Haven," she said, apparently eager to change the topic of conversation.

"I ran into Frieda Zimmerman at the market last weekend. She asked me to pass on her best wishes to you."

"Tell her I said hi when you see her again," she said, no doubt aware that he crossed paths with the elderly woman every week at the market.

"She also asked when you were coming home," he said.

It was what Kyle wanted to know, too, but he didn't want to admit that he missed her. Not only because he wasn't entirely comfortable with the realization, but also because he didn't want to put any additional pressure on her.

"I wish I knew," Erin finally said in answer to his question. "You have no idea how much I miss everyone in Haven."

"You mean you miss the food at The Home Station," he said, teasing to lighten the mood.

"And Jo's pizza," she acknowledged. "Although, your sister did send me a care package last week."

"So I heard," he said, not revealing that it had been his idea to send a box of frozen pizzas by overnight courier. "But pizza holds up better in transit than peppercorn-crusted New York striploin with garlic mashed potatoes and buttery green beans."

"I wouldn't know," she said. "No one has ever sent me peppercorn-crusted steak with potatoes and beans."

"Should I assume you've been living on Mini Wheats and PB and J sandwiches then?"

"No. My mom's a pretty good cook, and she's been making all my dad's favorite meals. Not that he has much of an appetite these days, but because she goes to the effort to cook, he forces himself to eat, which is important because he needs to keep up his strength."

"It's important for you, too," he said. "You won't be able to help take care of your dad if you don't take care of yourself."

"I'm taking care of myself," she promised. "But right now, I need to take care of the last cabin."

And with that, she signed off and he walked into the restaurant, still missing her.

Erin nearly jumped out of her skin when she walked into her bedroom after her shower the following Saturday night and found her brother Owen lounging on top of her bed. "What are you doing here?"

"I was looking for something to read," he told her.

She snatched the book out of his hand. "This is my bedroom, not a public library."

"But I knew you'd have an advanced copy of the newest Quinn Ellison book, and five pages in, I'm already hooked."

"Quinn will be happy to hear it. And I'll be happy to pass the book on to you *after* I've finished reading it," she promised. "Now get out so I can get to work."

He frowned at that as he rose to his feet. "It's almost ten o'clock."

"Okay, get out so I can go to sleep," she said.

"But you won't go to sleep, will you?"

She exhaled a weary sigh. "What do you want me to say, Owen?"

"I want you to say that you're taking care of yourself."

"I'm taking care of myself," she dutifully intoned.

He folded his arms over his chest. "Roger wasn't lying about the dark circles under your eyes—and they've only gotten worse over the past few weeks."

"The resort's been fully booked since Memorial Day weekend," she pointed out.

"You don't work at the resort," he reminded her.

"In case you haven't noticed, the family is a little short-staffed these days."

"Ian assured me that, between him and Nick, all of Dad's jobs are covered."

"They are," she confirmed.

"Which means that you're running yourself ragged covering for Anna," her brother guessed.

"Her pregnancy is really taking a toll," she said.

"Is that why she spent all day yesterday in town, lunching and shopping with Lisa Bodine?"

Erin frowned. "She went into town for a doctor's appointment."

"After which she had lunch and went shopping with Lisa."

She didn't question the truth of what he was saying—news traveled as far and fast in Silver Hook as it did in Haven. And though Owen had moved away a few years before she did, he still had friends in town who would be only too happy to share the latest gossip.

"What do you want me to say?" she asked instead.

"I don't want you to say anything—I want you to be pissed that she's taking advantage of you. And then tell Anna that you're not going to put up with it anymore."

Maybe she should be annoyed, but honestly, she was too tired to get worked up over the fact that her sister had played hooky for an afternoon—or even the past several weeks.

"Maybe it's time for you to go back to Haven," Owen said gently, when she failed to respond to his remark.

"What?" She was stunned by this suggestion. "Why?"

"Because Mom and Anna expect way too much of you."

"Marissa does more than I do," she pointed out. "And she's only part of the family through marriage."

"She also has a vested interested in this place, because she knows that it will belong to her and Ian someday."

"You mean when Dad decides to retire," she said, refusing to consider any other scenario in which her brother and sister-in-law would take over running the resort.

"When Dad retires," he confirmed.

But she saw the worry in his eyes—the same worry that weighed on her heart—and she knew that he didn't really believe the reassurance he'd offered her.

"In the meantime, I need to be here, Owen. Just for a little while longer."

He nodded slowly. "Okay."

She knew he understood, because Owen and Roger had been making the long trip from Portland every other weekend since their father's diagnosis, wanting to spend as much time as possible with Brian.

Just in case.

"Now get out of my room before I tell Mom," she said, teasing him with the threat she'd often used when they were kids.

"I'm going," he promised.

But first he wrapped his arms around her and hugged her tight.

She hugged him back, grateful for his love and support and offering him the same.

When he'd gone, Erin pushed aside her irritation with her sister and settled down to work.

But the following Saturday, when she was cleaning cabins again, she found herself wishing that she'd found a way to ask Anna to help. Even if her sister couldn't get down on her hands and knees to scrub the bathroom floor, she could at least wield a broom or a dusting cloth. Instead, Erin was tackling the chores on her own.

Again.

As she dragged the housekeeping cart toward Cabin Seven, she hesitated when she saw that the door was wide open.

Sometimes guests didn't bother to lock up when they checked out, but they usually at least closed the door.

Erin left her cart on the porch and cautiously peeked inside, aware that the local wildlife had been known to venture through any opening. The raccoons and chipmunks usually scurried out again quickly enough, but there had been an incident— back when she was in high school—when Cabin Four had been out of commission for a few weeks because a skunk had wandered in and was "surprised" by the return of the occupants.

Not a skunk, but a sloth, Erin noted—and immediately chastised herself for the uncharitable thought that popped into her head.

"Anna, what are you doing?"

"Earning my keep," her sister said, as she continued to sweep the kitchen area. "You always start at Cabin One, so I started at Twelve, knowing we'd meet in the middle."

Erin should be grateful for the help and leave it at that, but she was also a little concerned. "Are you sure you're not overdoing it?"

"It's my job," Anna reminded her. "And one I've been slacking off from for too long."

"But the doctor—"

"Assured me that moderate physical activity isn't just acceptable but recommended. He's also said that I'm getting fat."

"You're not getting fat," Erin denied, immediately rushing to her sister's defense. "And if he said that, maybe you should find another doctor."

"I've put on twelve pounds already," Anna confided. "And the doctor didn't actually use that word, but he did express concerned about the weight gain. And Owen expressed concern about you."

"Owen needs to mind his own business."

"Usually I wouldn't argue with that, but this time, he's right—you really do look like hell."

"Thanks for noticing," Erin said dryly.

"I should have noticed without my annoying brother pointing it out to me."

"And I always thought Ian was the annoying brother."

Anna smiled at that, then her expression turned serious again. "Since I found out I was pregnant, I've been so caught up in myself I haven't paid enough attention to what's going on around me, and I'm sorry for that. Sincerely."

"You don't need to be sorry. And you should be

focused on your baby—this is an exciting time for you and Nick."

"Exciting…and more than a little terrifying," her sister confided. "But we've got family around to help us navigate the rough spots, and I'm grateful for that. I'm grateful for *you*."

"I hate that I had to come home, but I'm glad to be here with you," she said, more than a little surprised to realize it was true.

"We'll see if you still think so in a few months when the baby hormones are making me completely crazy," Anna said.

"You mean that hasn't happened yet?" Erin teased.

And jumped back, laughing, as her sister took a swing at her with the broom.

Chapter Eight

Ten months later

"Have you heard from Erin?" Lucy asked from the doorway of Kyle's tiny office at The Home Station.

It was the tone of his sister's voice more than the words that set off his radar, tearing his attention away from the menu he was working on. "Not today," he said. "Did something happen with her dad?"

Lucy nodded. "He passed away early this morning."

He swore. "Did you talk to her?"

"Briefly."

"How's she doing?" he asked.

Lucy rubbed a hand over the swell of her belly. After more than two years of trying to get pregnant, his sister and brother-in-law were finally going to add to their family, their first baby being due in a little less than two months.

"She sounded okay, all things considered," she said in answer to his question.

Kyle pulled his phone out of his pocket and peeked at the call log, breathing a quiet sigh of relief to see that there was a missed call from Erin at 7:20 a.m., when he'd still been at the market. He was sorry to have missed her call, but he was also relieved to know that she'd reached out to him, as their communications had been growing more sporadic over the past several months.

In the beginning, they'd talked frequently and texted daily—sometimes several times a day. But as the weeks turned into months and her father's condition continued to deteriorate, their exchanges had become fewer and farther between. He understood that she was preoccupied, but recently she'd seemed even farther away than the geographical distance that separated them. Which made him wonder if she'd grown to regret the night they'd spent together—or maybe completely forgotten about it.

He wished he could forget, because more than eleven months later, he shouldn't still be dreaming about the one night they'd spent together. But dreaming about her was preferable to waking up alone and realizing how much he missed her.

Maybe part of the problem was that he hadn't slept with another woman since that night. He'd been out on a few dates, but he honestly hadn't wanted anything more. The idea of being with another woman—

or even kissing another woman—held less than zero appeal to him.

But why?

That was the question that nagged at him.

If he was a more romantic type, he might suspect that he'd fallen in love with Erin. But any illusions he'd had about romance had been destroyed along with his parents' marriage, so he knew he couldn't be in love with Erin and felt ridiculous for even contemplating the possibility.

Sure, what they'd shared was special—or at least more significant than a one-night stand. There had been an extra layer of intimacy to their lovemaking because of their friendship, and he'd decided that he was no longer willing to settle for anything less.

He also wished they'd had a chance to talk about what had happened between them—to clarify what it meant and didn't mean and to reestablish the boundaries of their relationship. Because they were friends. He genuinely enjoyed hanging out with her, talking about everything from books and movies to current events and political issues. And he loved cooking for her, because she was always so appreciative of the simplest things.

She'd once said that his Belgian waffles were like a taste of heaven. And when he'd let her sample a savory quiche recipe that he'd been experimenting with, she'd actually closed her eyes and moaned in a way that had his thoughts taking a quick detour from the kitchen to the bedroom.

"Kyle!"

He jolted. "What?"

Lucy shook her head. "Have you heard a single word I've said?"

"Sorry, I got so used to tuning you out when we were kids that it's become my default mode when you start rambling on," he said, because teasing her was preferable to admitting that his thoughts had wandered down a dangerous path.

"I wasn't rambling," she denied hotly.

"Then what were you saying?"

"I was saying, I know it's a lot to ask, but is there any chance that you'd be able to go to the funeral?"

"I'd already planned on it," he told her.

"You did?" She was obviously taken aback by his ready response.

"I mean, obviously I was hoping that there wouldn't need to be a funeral, but under the circumstances, yes, I figured I'd go. Especially since you're not in any condition to travel."

"I wish I could," Lucy said, sincerely regretful. "But you're right. Because of my sciatica, the doctor has advised against long road trips, and most airlines don't let pregnant women fly in their last trimester."

"Which is why I'm going," he said again, eager to reassure her.

"You don't think your boss will freak out about you being away from the restaurant for more than a day?" she asked.

Because she believed that Liam Gilmore was a taskmaster, not realizing that it was Kyle's choice to spend a hundred hours a week at the restaurant. And why not? He had nothing else to do with his time, and even less since Erin had been gone.

"We've had a few chats recently about work-life balance," Kyle told her now. "At Liam's initiative."

"Did he have to explain to you what that is?" she asked, only half teasing.

"I'm sure he won't mind if I take a few days off," he continued, ignoring her question. "Of course, that doesn't mean I won't be on the phone with the kitchen, but Giselle has proven that she's more than capable of taking the reins here."

"I have another request," Lucy said.

"You want bow ties with cheese sauce?" he guessed, naming the pasta she'd frequently asked him to make for her when they were younger and which had become a favorite again during her pregnancy.

She laughed. "No. Well, yes, if you're offering," she amended. "But I was thinking about your trip to Silver Hook."

"You want me to bring you back a T-shirt?"

"I want you to bring back Erin."

"I'm not sure that she'll want to leave her family the day after they bury her father," he pointed out.

"She might not want to leave at all," Lucy warned. "At least, that's my fear. She'll feel as if she needs to stay, to help out at the resort until her mom is steadier on her feet."

"That doesn't sound unreasonable."

"Except that every day she's there—and it's been almost a year now—she gets sucked deeper and deeper into a life she never wanted and tangled up in the demands of a family that doesn't appreciate her."

He wasn't going to argue with his sister about Erin's family or her relationship with them, but he was still uneasy about Lucy's request.

"I'll tell her that you want her to come home, but I'm not going to force the issue if it isn't what she wants."

"I thought you might say that," Lucy admitted. "That's why I'm sending backup."

"Backup?" he echoed curiously.

She nodded. "Quinn's going to Silver Hook with you."

Over the past few months, as her father's condition had continued to deteriorate, Erin had gotten through by focusing on one day at a time. When he finally took his last labored breath, she'd been overwhelmed by the sense of loss, but there had also been an inexplicable sense of relief. He'd fought hard, but the battle was finally over, and though she knew that she'd miss him forever, she also knew that he was in a better place, no longer in pain, finally at peace.

But when she went back to the house, where everyone had gathered after the final arrangements had been made, she realized that even in the midst of her family, she felt alone. Because while they were all dealing with the same loss, going through the same stages of grief, her mom had the support of all her children and Erin's siblings had their spouses, but she was on her own.

And she'd never felt so lonely.

Friends and neighbors stopped by to offer condolences and casseroles, sharing their favorite memories and fishing stories and expressing their regrets about a vibrant life abruptly cut short. The steady flow of people in and out of the house kept Bonnie occupied, allowing Erin some time to respond to the emails and text messages from her friends in Haven.

She'd reached out to Kyle, to tell him about her dad's passing, but her call had gone directly to voice mail. She didn't try again. Over the past few months, they'd fallen out of touch—her fault, she knew, but limiting her contact with Kyle had been the only way she'd been able to deal with everything that was happening at the time. Instead, she'd dialed Lucy's number next, and had nearly lost it completely when she heard her friend's voice.

But it was okay, because Lucy cried right along with her, and for a moment, it was almost as if her best friend was there. Of course, Lucy was in her seventh month of pregnancy, so there was no way she'd be able to make the trip to Silver Hook, and Erin wouldn't have expected her to even if she could, but it was a comfort to know that she cared.

She'd talked to Quinn later that day, too, and promised her friend that they'd get together to catch up as soon as Erin got back to Haven—whenever that might be.

Today, facing two visitations—from 10:00 to 12:00 and 2:00 to 4:00—she found herself wishing that she'd asked her friend to come. And tomorrow, the day of the funeral, she knew would be even worse. A time to say her last goodbye to her father, her friend and confidant, her champion. He was the one person who'd always been in her corner. The one she'd been most reluctant to leave when she moved to Haven—and the one who'd insisted that she go. Because he'd understood that she needed to move away to build a career that had nothing to do with catching, gutting or frying fish and a life in which she was valued for herself.

The last guests from the early visitation left just after noon, which meant that the family had a little less than two hours to recharge their batteries before they had to do it all again at two.

Ian and Marissa decided to take advantage of the break and take their girls out for a bite to eat, promising to bring something back for Mom, who was going over the details for the next day's service with Owen and the funeral director. Anna and Nick had taken Nicky, their now five-month-old son, outside for some fresh air, and Erin thought that she should probably go outside, too, but she didn't have enough energy to walk even that far. Instead, she dropped onto one of the sofas in the family lounge.

"There's my two favorite guys," she said, when Roger walked into the room with his eight-week-old nephew tucked in the crook of his arm like a football.

"Joel needed a diaper change," he said, dropping the tote bag stuffed with baby supplies at her feet. "But I took care of it."

"Look at you, daddy-in-training," she teased.

"Owen told you that we're thinking about having a baby," he guessed.

She nodded. "He said you've got an appointment with an adoption agency next month."

"Do you think we're crazy?"

"No." She shook her head. "I think you guys will be awesome parents."

"We'll do our best," he promised. "In the meantime, we'll continue practicing our skills on the newest addition to the family." He reached out with his free hand and linked his fingers with hers. "How are you holding up?"

"On a wing and a prayer," she admitted.

"I'm not surprised," he said. "You've been on your feet all day."

"So have you," she pointed out.

"But I'm not wearing three-inch heels."

"They were the only dress shoes I brought," she said. "Which makes me wonder what I was thinking when I packed."

"I'd guess you were thinking that you wanted to get home and just grabbed whatever you put your hands on and shoved it in your suitcase."

"That pretty much sums it up."

"In which case, you really lucked out with that dress," he said, referring to the simple black sheath she was wearing. "You make grief look gorgeous."

She managed a small smile. "It's not mine," she confided. "I borrowed it from Anna's closet."

"Does she know?"

"She offered it to me, confessing that she can't

squeeze into it right now, anyway, because her boobs are so much bigger than mine."

"Gloating, you mean?" he guessed.

She shrugged. "I was just happy that I didn't have to go shopping for a dress."

Roger tilted his head, listening as the distant voices in the hall drew nearer. "Sounds like our quiet space is about to get less quiet."

Before she could respond, Owen appeared in the doorway.

"There's someone here to see you, Erin."

Her brother's words were little more than a buzz in her ears as her gaze shifted to the man standing behind him.

"Is that… Kyle?" Roger whispered the question to her.

She managed a nod as he stepped into the lounge.

His gaze shifted from Erin to the man beside her and back again.

Roger let go of the hand she hadn't realized he was still holding and smoothly rose to his feet without disturbing the sleeping baby tucked in the crook of his arm. "I'm Roger Howard—Erin's brother-in-law."

Kyle's puzzled expression cleared as he shook the proffered hand. "Kyle Landry. A friend of Erin's from Haven."

She summoned the energy to push herself off the couch, her bruised and battered heart filling with happiness and gratitude, mixed with more than a little bit of panic.

"Kyle." Tears filled her eyes, clogged her throat.

She hadn't spoken to him in weeks and though she knew Lucy would have shared the news about her dad, she'd never anticipated that he would show up in Silver Hook. Unprepared for his appearance now, her panicked gaze darted from him to the baby in her brother-in-law's arms and back again. "What are you doing here?"

"I thought you could use a friend."

"You have no idea how much," she confided.

He opened his arms and she stepped into his embrace willingly. Gratefully. And more than a little warily.

"Well, you've got two here now from Haven," he told her.

"Two?" she said, uncomprehending.

"Quinn came with me, but she got caught up on a call with her editor so I left her outside because I didn't want to wait another minute to see you."

She leaned into his chest, breathing in his familiar scent, absorbing the comfort of his arms around her.

"We'll, uh, give you two some privacy," Roger said, nudging his husband toward the door.

Erin didn't object. While she didn't think that Owen knew about her hookup with Kyle—she trusted Roger had kept her confidence—the way her brother was eyeing the newcomer warned her that it wouldn't take him long to put the pieces together.

"But we'll be right next door, if you need anything," Owen said.

"Thanks."

"I'm so sorry about your dad," Kyle said when they were alone.

"He didn't have an easy go of it," she said—an obvious understatement. "But now I picture him at the pearly gates, asking if there's any good crappie fishing in heaven."

"Isn't good crappie an oxymoron?"

She surprised herself by laughing at his question. "C-r-a-p-p-i-e. It's a type of sunfish, which I'm sure you know because it's readily available in Nevada, too."

"Yeah, I know," he admitted. "I just wanted to make you smile."

"And you did," she confirmed.

"I've missed you."

"I've missed you, too. And Lucy and Claudio and Quinn."

"Lucy wanted to be here," he told her now. "But her doctor didn't want her traveling so close to her due date."

Erin nodded. "But she's okay?"

"She's doing great," Kyle assured her. "Eager for the baby to be born—and hoping you'll be back in Haven before that happens."

She hesitated, unwilling to commit to anything just yet. "I don't know what my plans are," she finally said. "For the past few months, I've just been focused on getting through one day at a time."

"That's understandable," he said.

A knock sounded on the open door. "Sorry to interrupt," Roger said, poking his head into the room again. "But this little guy is starting to fuss and I can't find a bottle."

"In the fridge," Erin said, already moving toward the kitchenette part of the lounge.

She took the bottle out and set it in a plastic bowl in the sink, filling the bowl with hot water from the tap to warm the milk.

"Do you want me to feed him?" Roger asked.

"No, I've got it," Erin said, taking the fussy baby from him.

"You're sure?"

She nodded, and Roger slipped out of the room again.

"I'm guessing this is your nephew," Kyle said, eyeing the baby in her arms.

"My nephew?" she echoed.

"Isn't that Nicky—Anna and Nick's baby?" he prompted.

"Oh. Um. No. This is… Joel."

His brows drew together. "Whose baby is he?"

She swallowed. "Mine."

Chapter Nine

Kyle felt his jaw hit the floor.

Erin had a baby?

When the hell had *that* happened?

And why had she kept it a secret?

As these questions swirled in his mind, a trickle of unease slid down his spine. "How old is he?"

Erin drew in a breath, as if bracing herself for a difficult admission. "Eight and a half weeks."

Just over two months.

Which meant...

He took a closer look at the baby. "You said his name's Joel?"

She nodded as she took the bottle out of the warm water and shook a few drops of milk onto the inside of her wrist to test its temperature. "Joel Brian Landry."

Kyle felt dizzy, as if the whole world had suddenly been turned upside down.

"Joel for your mom and Brian… for my dad," she explained, a hint of emotion in her voice.

He was feeling pretty emotional, too. "And Landry because he's…mine."

Though it wasn't a question, she nodded anyway.

He was stunned.

And furious.

And—perhaps most unexpectedly—he felt a surge of pride that he'd played a part, however small, in creating the baby in her arms.

Which didn't make any sense, because a child hadn't been part of his plan. But the plan didn't seem to matter so much now that he was faced with the reality of a baby.

His baby.

"Say something. Please," Erin urged, as she offered the bottle to the infant, who immediately latched on to the nipple and began suckling.

"I don't know where to begin," he admitted.

There were so many questions spinning around in his head he couldn't seem to grab hold of any one.

And while it was obvious that he and Erin needed to talk, he recognized that this was neither the time nor the place—especially not when friends and neighbors would start arriving any minute now for the visitation because her father had just died.

So he was both frustrated and relieved to acknowledge that the conversation they needed to have would have to wait. Because as much as he wanted answers right now, he also needed some time to absorb the impact of her revelation.

He had a child.

An eight-and-a-half-week-old son.

Which meant that he'd already missed out on the first two months of the little guy's life, and no way was he going to miss any more. *He* wasn't going to abandon his child like his own father had done.

Joel Brian Landry.

Repeating the name inside his head, Kyle discovered that he liked it.

And he was grateful that Erin had given their son his surname, recognizing the gesture as confirmation that she hadn't intended to keep the baby's existence a secret from him forever, even if she'd done so for the whole of her pregnancy and two months after.

"Erin?" A thirtysomething woman in a long-sleeved black dress hovered in the doorway. "I'm sorry to interrupt, but your mom wanted you to know that visitors are starting to arrive."

"Thanks, Marissa. You can tell her that I'll be out as soon as I've finished feeding Joel," Erin promised.

"We'll talk after," Kyle said.

Again, it wasn't a question, but she nodded.

He exited the lounge so that she could finish tending to the baby—*his baby!*—without any distractions.

He met Quinn at the main doors as she was on her way in.

"What did I miss?" she asked.

He didn't know where to begin.

* * *

The past few months, Erin felt as if her life had truly been a roller coaster. There were so many highs and lows—and days when she felt as if she'd never get off the ride. Today had brought new heights: seeing Quinn again and finally getting to introduce Kyle to his son; and depths: having to face the reality that her dad was truly and forever gone.

And the roller coaster wasn't done yet. After the visitation, Quinn had tried to sneak off to check into The Lucky Angler so that Erin and Kyle would have some time to talk privately, but Erin couldn't let her friends stay at a motel when there were empty cabins at Sunfish Bay.

If her dad had held on for another few weeks, the resort would have been fully booked, but it was early enough in the spring that there were still a few vacant cabins. Ian was certain their father had planned it that way, so that they would be done with the funeral and all the mourning before the height of the season. Erin didn't doubt he was right. Brian Napper had never wanted anything to interfere with the business.

Now they were finally back at the resort, inside Cabin Ten—a two-bedroom unit with spectacular views of the lake in the daytime. Despite the fact that darkness would soon be falling, Quinn had insisted on taking a flashlight and going for a walk, and now that Joel had been fed and was asleep again, Erin knew there was no more avoiding the conversation that she and Kyle needed to have.

"This is a great place your family has," he began.

"It is, isn't it?" she agreed. "Growing up here, I took it for granted, but now when I come back, I can appreciate everything the resort has to offer.

"At least for the first few days," she clarified. "Then I remember how much work it is. Twelve cabins means there are a lot of beds to make."

"And toilets to clean," he said.

She managed a small smile. "I think we can move past the small talk now, so why don't you just ask what you want to ask?"

He nodded. "Okay. Let's start with—why didn't you tell me?"

"I was going to tell you."

"When?" he demanded.

"When I came back to Haven," she said.

Kyle shook his head, clearly unsatisfied with her response. "He's two months old, Erin. You've had two months—and nine months before that—to say something. But you didn't."

"We spent one night together. We took precautions. I'm sorry that I didn't immediately realize I'd skipped a period and think, 'I better call Kyle because I might be pregnant.'"

"But there obviously came a point when you realized 'might be' had changed to 'am,'" he pointed out. "And yet my phone didn't ring."

"By that time, I hadn't talked to you in a few weeks," she confided, "and when I spoke with Lucy, I found out that you were dating Shirla Lawrie—"

"It was one date," he said, frustrated to think that was her justification for keeping him in the dark.

"I didn't know that," she said, imploring him to understand. "And you made your feelings about unplanned pregnancies perfectly clear when you accused my sister of trapping Nick into marriage."

He winced at the reminder of that long-ago conversation. "Nick and Anna aren't you and me."

"No," she agreed. "They were actually in a relationship and in love with one another. We're just friends who spent one night together."

"Which might have turned into something more if you hadn't left town the very next day." Even as the words spilled out of his mouth, he wished he could take them back.

Her eyes went wide and she took an instinctive step back, as if to retreat from the pain his callous response had caused. "I had to go," she reminded him, her tone noticeably cooler now. "My dad was sick. Dying."

"I know," he acknowledged, sincerely contrite.

"But even if I hadn't left," she continued, "we both know that one night wouldn't have turned into anything more because you've never wanted anything more. Every time you broke up with one of your numerous girlfriends, you reiterated that you had no interest in getting married or having a family, so forgive me for not being eager to share the news that I was having your baby after you'd made it clear that you didn't ever want to be a father."

He wondered how it was that she was the one

who'd kept a secret for eleven months, but he was suddenly the one on the defensive.

"Regardless of anything I said or did, you should have reached out when you knew you were pregnant," he said. "Or, failing that, when the baby was born. I shouldn't have had to find out—more than two months later—only because I showed up on your doorstep."

"You're right," she agreed. "And the day he was born, I called you from the hospital."

He frowned. "No, you didn't."

"Yes, I did," she insisted. "I forgot to calculate the time difference and called during dinner rush at the restaurant, but you said you'd get back to me later. Instead, you texted in the early hours of the morning to apologize because you'd gone out with some of the staff for a drink after closing and forgot to call."

He winced. "So you decided to punish me by not telling me about my child?"

"No," she immediately denied, then sighed. "I don't know. Maybe. It was an emotional day. I had all these hormones in my system, so many feelings churning inside that I desperately wanted to share with you. But I hadn't seen you in nine months, and I realized that, in that time, you'd moved on with your life. And I didn't want to interfere with that by making you feel responsible for me or my baby."

"But I am responsible. He's my child, too."

"I've never denied that."

"Except that you just did, Erin. You referred to him as *your* baby, not *our* baby." He scrubbed his hands over his face. "I'm sorry. This is all just…a lot. I know this is a difficult day for you, and I'm making it harder." He was quiet for a minute, trying to sort out his thoughts. "Okay, let's talk logistics."

"Logistics?" she echoed warily.

He nodded. "I think it makes sense to clear the desk out of my office and make it into a room for the baby. I'll get a crib and change table and whatever else he needs. Just make a list, and I'll take care of it."

"It's great that you want to make space for Joel, but you're getting ahead of yourself a little," Erin said. "He won't be going anywhere for overnight visits until he's weaned, and that isn't likely to happen for another four months."

"I don't want overnight visits," he said. "I want you and Joel to live with me."

She immediately shook her head. "I appreciate your willingness to upend your life—or at least your home office—but we're not moving in with you. Once everything is settled here, we'll move back to my apartment where you can spend as much time with him as you want."

"You sublet your apartment nine months ago," he reminded her.

"And Shawna's moving out at the end of the month. She already gave me her notice."

"The end of the month isn't for another seven days, and I've already missed the first two months of his life."

"As if you wouldn't have spent most of that time at the restaurant anyway," she shot back.

He couldn't deny that was probably true. Since The Home Station had opened, Kyle could be found in the kitchen there more often than anywhere else. And while he'd never be able to work a regular eight-hour shift in the restaurant business, he knew it was possible to cut back his hours—he'd just never had a reason before.

Now that he knew he had a child, he had a reason.

Before he could share that thought with Erin, though, there was a knock on the door and Quinn poked her head into the cabin. "Is it safe to come in? It's starting to rain and a flashlight isn't very effective as an umbrella."

"Of course," Erin said, gesturing for her to enter.

"Maybe you can talk some sense into your friend," Kyle grumbled.

"You know, a little rain never hurt anyone," Quinn said, turning back toward the door.

"Don't go," Erin said, shooting a glare at Kyle. "We're just having a little disagreement about the timeline for my return to Haven."

"If you fly back to Nevada with me and Quinn on Friday, you'll have two extra sets of hands to help with the baby and all his stuff."

"I can't leave my family the day after the funeral," she protested. "Not to mention that if I flew, I wouldn't have my car when we got back to Haven, and I'd need it to sleep in because Shawna isn't moving out of my apartment until next week."

"You can stay with me," he said.

"It makes a lot more sense for me to drive back at the end of the month."

"I don't like the idea of you driving sixteen hundred miles alone," Kyle admitted.

"I did it eleven months ago," she pointed out to him.

"And I didn't like the idea then, either," he reminded her. "But I knew I couldn't stop you."

"And you can't stop me now."

"It's a long drive for anyone to undertake on their own," Quinn said, attempting to play peacemaker. "And probably even more so with a baby."

"She's right," Kyle said. "If you insist on staying until the end of the month, I'll fly out here again and drive back with you."

"I'm not sure your boss would be happy about you taking another three days off next week."

"Liam will understand."

"Maybe," she said. "But it's not necessary. And truthfully, I'm not sure it's a good idea for you and me to be stuck in a car together for a twenty-five hour trip."

"I've got a better idea," Quinn said. "I'll stay here until Erin's ready to leave and then I'll drive back with her."

"Don't you have a deadline in a few weeks?" Erin asked her friend.

"I do, but I've also got my laptop with me."

"I think it's reasonable compromise," Kyle said.

Plus, Quinn's offer ensured that Erin couldn't renege on her promise to return to Haven at the end of the month. Not to mention that the presence of friend at the resort would provide something of a buffer between Erin and her family.

Kyle had only exchanged a few words with each of her mom and siblings at the funeral home, but he'd observed their interactions with one another. And maybe it wasn't fair to judge, considering the heightened emotions of everyone at present, but it seemed that, even in the midst of their grief, Erin was somehow relegated to the background.

When Lucy had asked him to bring her friend back to Haven, he'd refused to make any promises, understanding that Erin would need some time with her family to grieve and figure out her next steps. He'd even considered the unhappy possibility that she might want to stay in Silver Hook, close to her mom and siblings.

Now that he knew she'd had his baby, that was no longer an option.

The morning after the funeral, Kyle left early for the airport and his return flight to Nevada, and Quinn was hanging out in the cabin with her laptop, leaving Erin alone with her thoughts—at least until her sister-in-law sat down across from her at the dining room table.

"Is everything okay?" Marissa asked gently.

"You mean aside from the fact that we buried Dad yesterday?" Erin asked.

Her sister-in-law smiled gently. "Yeah, aside from that."

Erin shook her head. "No."

"You're dealing with a lot," Marissa noted sympathetically. "In addition to grieving for your dad and supporting your mom, you've got all those baby hormones messing with your equilibrium."

"And Kyle pressuring me to go back to Haven."

"Isn't that what you want, too?"

"It is," she acknowledged. "I just think, with everything that's happened, the timing isn't right for me to leave."

"You're worried about Bonnie."

"If I go back to Haven—"

"*When* you go back to Haven," her sister-in-law interjected.

"—she'll be alone."

"No, she won't," Marissa reminded her. "Anna and Nick and Nicky will be living here until construction on their house is finished, and me and Ian and Amie and Ella are less than five miles down the road. Not to mention the guests who will be in and out of the resort all summer. She will *not* be alone."

Erin nodded a reluctant acknowledgment.

"So there's no reason for you to stay," her sister-in-law continued.

"I know. But I can't help wondering…what Dad would want me to do."

"He'd want you to go," Bonnie said from the doorway. "He never wanted you to come home in the first place."

The combination of her words and the harshness of her tone made Erin feel as if she'd been slapped.

"Don't say something you're going to regret," Marissa gently cautioned her mother-in-law.

"She was wondering what her father would want her to do, and I told her."

Erin should have left it at that, but apparently she had a streak of masochism, because she asked, "What do *you* want, Mom?"

Bonnie didn't hesitate. "I want you to go back to Haven."

Chapter Ten

It was later than Erin had anticipated when she finally pulled into her designated parking spot at the triplex that had been her home for four years prior to her return to Silver Hook. And though she'd been gone for eleven months, her heart filled with an unexpected sense of rightness and peace when she saw the glow of lights through the windows of her living room.

Kyle's doing, she guessed.

He was undoubtedly still furious with her for not telling him when she found out she was pregnant. Nevertheless, he'd put the lights on so that she wouldn't walk into a dark apartment with their baby.

She felt the telltale sting of tears behind her eyes and had a sudden urge to drop her head onto the steering wheel and cry, even if she didn't know why. Of course, after the emotional ups and downs of the past year, she didn't ever seem to need a specific reason for the tears to start.

Baby hormones, Anna claimed, and Erin was willing to acknowledge that those were at least part of it.

"We're home," she whispered the announcement to her sleeping son as she shifted into Park and turned off the ignition.

Of course, as soon as the subtle vibrations of the engine stopped, Joel woke up and immediately started fussing.

"I know you're tired of being strapped in that car seat," she said soothingly. "So let's get you upstairs, then I'll come back and get your Pack 'n Play. You can sleep in there tonight—and we'll go to the baby store to pick up your crib tomorrow."

She probably should have asked Kyle to pick it up for her—she was definitely going to have to ask for his help to put it together—but for tonight, the playpen would suffice.

She draped the diaper bag over her shoulder, then unlatched the car seat from its anchored base and headed up the stairs to her second-floor apartment.

Before she could slide her key into the lock, the door opened from the other side.

"I was watching for you," Kyle said, offering the explanation in lieu of a greeting. "Quinn texted when you dropped her off in Cooper's Corners, so I knew it would only take you about twenty minutes to get home from there."

"Twenty minutes after twenty-eight hours," she noted.

"That's a long drive," he acknowledged.

"Made longer by the fact that we had to stop every few hundred miles," she said. "Joel usually loves riding in the car, but I guess the extended journey was a little too much for him. Thankfully I had Quinn to share the driving with me, or it might have taken us three days to get home."

"I'll bet the trip was hard on you, too," he said. "How are you feeling?"

She was touched that he asked, pleased that he cared, and that was enough to make her want to blubber again. But she managed to hold it together—at least for the moment.

"I'm okay," she said. "Tired. Hungry."

"How does tagliatelle with asparagus and parmesan fonduta sound?" he asked.

"Heavenly." She sniffed the air. "Is that what I smell?"

He nodded. "It was one of tonight's features at The Home Station."

She lost the battle now and her eyes filled with tears. "I didn't expect this. I don't know what to say."

"You don't have to say anything," he told her. "Just have a seat while I dish up your dinner."

"Will it keep another twenty minutes?" she asked, lifting the baby out of the carrier. "I need to change and feed Joel before I worry about filling my own belly."

"It'll keep," he said.

"And I need to bring up his playpen from the car, so that he has somewhere to sleep tonight."

"About that," he said, taking her arm and steering her down the hall. "I hope I haven't overstepped, but—"

He pushed open the door of what had previously been a spare bedroom to reveal a freshly painted and fully furnished nursery. The crib, change table, dresser and glider rocker were dark wood that contrasted beautifully with walls of a soft sage green decorated with decals of all the characters from the Hundred Acre Wood.

Erin felt the sting of fresh tears as she looked around, marveling at the obvious care and attention to detail that had gone into making the room over for their baby.

"Shawna only moved out on Tuesday," she remarked. "When did you do all this?"

"I reached out to her when I got back from Silver Hook, to tell her what I wanted to do, so she let me in on the weekend to ensure the paint would have time to cure before you got home with the baby."

"It's...perfect," she told him.

"So you're not going to ask me to give your key back?"

"I'm not going to ask for my key," she confirmed. "In fact, I was thinking—in the spirit of compromise and cooperation—to lift the 'emergency use' only condition. I'm not saying you should just walk in at all hours, but if you want to see Joel and I don't respond to your knock on the door, you should feel free to let yourself in because I'm probably just busy with the baby."

"Thank you," he said.

"Thank *you* for doing such a fabulous job with this room."

"You'll have to thank Claudio and Lucy, too," he warned. "Because they helped."

"I guess that means they know…about Joel?"

"Yeah. I needed another set of hands to assemble the crib, so I asked Claudio to stop by, but I didn't tell him why. Of course, Lucy insisted on tagging along and…well, she didn't have too much trouble figuring things out when she saw what I was doing."

"Is she mad?" Erin asked warily, setting the baby on top of the fully stocked change table and unsnapping his sleeper.

"That you had a baby?"

"That I didn't tell her," she clarified, briskly swapping out the baby's wet diaper for a clean one.

"You've got some explaining to do," he warned. "But I don't think she'll stay mad for long. She's already convinced that our baby and her baby aren't just going to be cousins but best friends."

"That was always Lucy's plan," Erin acknowledged with a smile as she refastened the sleeper. "Not that our kids would be cousins—I don't think she ever imagined *that*—but that they'd grow up together and be best friends."

"Well, she's excited to meet her nephew, although I swore her to secrecy because I didn't want my mom to hear from anyone but us that she's a grandma."

"You haven't told her yet?" Erin asked, surprised.

"Considering the tension in our relationship, I decided it would be best to wait until she could actually meet the baby, fall head over heels in love with him and immediately forgive me for everything I've ever done wrong."

Erin chuckled softly. "Those are some pretty lofty expectations for a first meeting," she noted. "Joel's a cute kid, but he's not magic."

While Erin was tending to the baby, Kyle brought up the suitcases, boxes and various other paraphernalia from her car. He had to make several trips, depositing most of the items just inside the door before returning to her vehicle again. But the last box was filled with Joel's toys, so he carried that directly into the nursery—where she was still feeding the baby.

He halted abruptly and ordered himself to look away. To look anywhere but at the breast being suckled by their infant son.

But while breasts were undeniably one of Kyle's favorite female body parts, the feeling that rushed through his veins as he watched Erin nurse their baby was emotional rather than sexual. And the beautiful image of mother and child was one that he knew would be imprinted on his memory forever.

He'd only been partly joking when he'd expressed hope that his mother would be so captivated by her firstborn grandchild she'd willingly forgive all of the father's transgressions, because the truth was, meeting his son for the first time had tempered some of Kyle's hurt and anger that Erin had kept their child's existence from him. And a little more of his lingering resentment melted now, washed away by a wave of gratitude for everything that she'd done to nurture and care for their son, not just in the two months since he'd been born, but throughout the whole of her pregnancy.

Erin glanced up then and spotted him hovering in the doorway. "You can come in," she said. "Any modesty I might have had was left behind in the delivery room."

He accepted the invitation and set the box of toys on the floor beside the dresser. "I was going to tell you that I want to help out as much as possible with Joel, but I guess there are some things I can't do."

"I do pump sometimes and freeze the milk, so that I can give him a bottle when it's not convenient to nurse," she said.

"Like at the funeral home," he realized.

She nodded. "Though that was more a restriction of the dress than the location—and why I was so desperate to nurse him when we finally got back to Sunfish Bay. But I'd be happy to pump more frequently so that you can feed him, if it's something you want to do."

"It is," he said. "But you'll have to show me how. I don't have a lot—or actually any—experience with babies."

"I can show you," she promised, easing the baby from her breast and lifting him to her shoulder.

She held him with one hand on his back while the other closed the cup of her nursing bra and then adjusted her shirt to cover it, before rising to her feet and handing the baby off to him.

"He doesn't fuss around strangers, does he?" he asked, eyeing the baby with some trepidation, certain he would balk at the stiffness of his dad's hold and start to scream in protest.

"You're not a stranger—you're his dad," Erin said easily.

"But he doesn't know that," Kyle felt compelled to point out.

"Sure he does," she disagreed, as she laid a cloth over his shoulder.

A burp cloth, he knew, having experienced the result of holding a recently fed baby without the protection of one when he was in Silver Hook for her dad's funeral.

"I talk to Joel about you all the time," she told him now.

"You do?"

She nodded. "Even before he was born, I talked to him about how I hoped he—or she, because I didn't know his sex—would have your green-gray eyes, your patience and kindness and sense of humor. And after he was born, I promised that I'd bring him to Haven as soon as I could, so that he could meet you. I told him that he'd recognize you, because you have strong hands but a gentle touch and you always smell like lime and basil."

He was flattered by the description, and a little bemused. "I don't smell like lime and basil."

"You do," she insisted. "It's the hand soap you use at the restaurant. I ordered the same soap for my bathroom at Sunfish Bay."

"You did?"

"I like the scent and...it reminded me of you."

"I've been trying to stay mad at you," he confessed, as he gently patted the baby's back. "But the more we talk, the more I'm starting to believe that you did what you thought was best under very difficult circumstances."

"I never wanted to deprive you of knowing your son. I just didn't know if you'd want to know."

"You used to say that you could talk to me about anything," he reminded her.

"And when I talked to you about Anna and Nick, you warned that my brother-in-law might end up resenting his wife and their baby because the pregnancy forced them to move up their wedding date."

"Well, I said you should have talked to me, not that you should have listened to me."

She managed a smile then. "I'm going to go have my pasta now. Joel's asleep, by the way, if you want to put him in his crib."

Kyle shook his head. "I have a lot of lost time to make up for, so I'm going to hold him for a while, if that's okay."

"Of course, it's okay," she said. "And I'd be happy

to call you when he wakes up at three a.m., if you want to make up for lost time then."

"You wouldn't have to call me if you moved into my apartment," he pointed out.

"Didn't we have this conversation already?"

"Yeah," he admitted. "But I was hoping you'd change your mind."

"I appreciate that you want to be involved. Sincerely. And I promise, you can spend as much time as you want with Joel. But I don't see any benefits—and a whole bunch of potential pitfalls—of us living together."

He started to argue the point, but they'd already argued too much. At least she was back in Haven, which was a helluva lot better than sixteen hundred miles away in Silver Hook.

So why did it still feel as if she was still far away when he could see her standing on the other side of the room?

Maybe he was expecting too much. Yes, they'd previously been close friends who'd shared an easy camaraderie and genuine affection, and now there was distance and suspicion. But she'd been gone for almost a year, and she'd been through a lot in that time, culminating in the loss of her father after an extended illness but also including a pregnancy and childbirth.

Of course, that was her choice. If she'd told him about the baby, he would have been there. Yeah, he probably would have freaked out at first—as he did freak out inside when he realized that she'd had a child—but once he got over the shock and worked through the instinctive denial, he would have been there.

He wasn't ever going to walk out on his child like his father had walked out on his. And he was going to be there for Erin, too—whether she wanted him to be or not.

"You're practically falling asleep on your feet," he noted, as she pushed the remnants of her pasta around on her plate.

"It's been a really long two days," she acknowledged.

For him, too, waiting for her to make the six-teen-hundred-mile journey and finally bring his son home. But he knew better than to compare his anticipation with her actual physical exhaustion.

"I'll put Joel in his crib then head out so you can get some sleep, too."

After the baby was settled, Erin followed Kyle to the door. "Thank you again. For everything."

"Welcome home," he said and, giving in to his own need, drew her into his arms.

Chapter Eleven

Having a baby changed everything, Erin mused, as she settled her son at her breast. Before Joel was born, she fantasized about sandy beaches and blue waters and fruity drinks. Now her fantasies were all about sleep. Twelve hours of uninterrupted slumber was the ultimate dream; she would have settled for six. Unfortunately, Joel was a growing boy who was still waking several times in the night, which meant that she was lucky if she managed to get three before she was awakened by his demands to be fed again.

And yet, she felt pretty good when she woke up at 6:00 a.m. the morning following her late return to Haven. She was happy to be back in her own place, and maybe relieved, too. She felt as if she and Kyle had made some good progress the night before, and though they still had a lot to talk about, she was optimistic that they would be able to work together for the benefit of their son.

After she fed the baby—yet again—she spent a few extra minutes pumping to add to the store of milk in the freezer, cognizant of Kyle's interest in being able to give their baby a bottle. Some of the books she'd read had warned about the possibility of nipple confusion for babies who were switched between breast and bottle, but thankfully Joel didn't seem to be bothered. As long as his tummy was being filled, he was a happy baby.

When he went down for his morning nap, Erin decided to tackle the unpacking. She'd just tucked her suitcases away in the closet when her phone chimed to indicate receipt of a text message. She swiped the screen. It was from Anna—We miss you!—along with a video of Nicky blowing kisses—with his mom's help, of course.

She'd grown closer to her sister during the eleven months that she'd been in Silver Hook—and it had been a happy surprise to both of them to discover that they'd become friends. Roger was still Erin's absolute favorite of her siblings and their partners, but Anna had moved into a solid second place.

Roger and Anna were also the only members of her family who hadn't badgered Erin about the identity of the baby's father as soon as her pregnancy was revealed. Roger because she'd told him about the night she'd spent with Kyle, so he'd figured it out pretty quickly; Anna because she'd figured it out, too, despite having less information.

"Why haven't you asked me about the baby's father?" Erin asked when she was shopping with Anna one day in preparation for the arrival of her sister's baby.

"I don't have to ask," Anna had said confidently. "Because I know."

"You think so?" Erin challenged, certain that she didn't.

"I might not always be the most perceptive person, but not even I could miss the sparks zinging between you and your chef friend the night that Nick and I had dinner at your apartment."

She swallowed. "You think Kyle's the father?"

Her sister folded her arms over her chest. "Are you really going to tell me that he isn't?"

"No," Erin finally admitted.

"So...does he know?"

She shook her head.

"Are you going to tell him?"

"Eventually."

"Why not now?"

"Because right now, my life is here and his is in Haven, and I don't want him to feel guilty about the fact that he can't be here with me."

Assuming that he'd want to be there, which was admittedly a very big assumption on her part.

And maybe that was one of the reasons that she hadn't been eager to tell him about the baby—because she'd been afraid to find out that he *didn't* want to be there. That he wouldn't be excited to learn that they were going to have a baby after only one night together. That he'd reject their child as her mother had rejected her.

She'd forgotten that Kyle had some experience with rejection, too. That his dad had chosen another woman over his mom, and the children he had with his second wife over Kyle and Lucy. Which was, she realized now, likely a very big part of the reason that Kyle was determined to be there for his child, to prove that he wasn't like his father.

And if she'd considered that possibility when she was pregnant—or even when Joel was born—she might have been brave enough to share her joy and excitement and even her fears with the father of her child.

She sighed softly as she settled into the rocking chair with the baby. "Oh, Joel. What have I done?"

Of course, there was no response to her question, though he did tip his head back to look at her with a wide-eyed curiosity that assured her he was interested in her thoughts, even if he couldn't hold up his end of the conversation.

She took his hands in hers and showed him how to stretch his arms out in front, then spread them wide and lift them over his head. He smiled, loving the attention.

"I thought I was doing the right thing, keeping the news of the pregnancy to myself, but my thoughts were so tangled up with emotions, I wasn't sure where one ended and another began."

She clapped his hands together, finding joy in the simple act of playing with her son despite the ache in her heart. "And I guess, in the end, whatever reasons and rationale I used to justify not telling your dad are irrelevant now. Because of the choices I made, he missed out on the first eight-and-a-half weeks of your life."

But even if she'd told him as soon as she'd discovered that she was pregnant, she couldn't imagine that anything would have been different. The sixteen hundred mile distance between Silver Hook and Haven wasn't something that was open to discussion or negotiation—it just was. And while Erin had to be in Arkansas because her dad was sick, everything that mattered to Kyle was in Nevada.

"I could have talked to him, though," she acknowledged now, continuing to clap Joel's hands together as she spoke aloud, as the experts recommended, in order to encourage his efforts at communication. "And even if he couldn't have been there, I could have sent him a copy of your first ultrasound photo or even the audio file of your heartbeat. I could have found a way to let him be a part of it."

And she'd wanted to, but so many times when she'd been tempted enough to reach for her phone to call, she'd heard the echo of his words in the back of her mind.

"...he's going to resent both her and the baby."

Yes, he'd been talking about Anna and Nick, but their situation was the same, and she didn't ever want

Kyle to think that she would use a child to try to hold on to him.

In all the years that she'd known him, he'd been involved in more than a few romantic relationships that had fallen apart because cooking was his passion and his priority and would always take precedence over any woman he dated. And because she'd been witness to those sorrows, she hadn't been looking for a relationship when she invited him to her bed—and she'd be a fool to look for one now. Because nothing had changed in the past twelve months.

Nothing except that they had a child now, which pretty much guaranteed that they were going to be in one another's lives for at least the next eighteen years as they raised their son together while living separate and apart. Co-parenting was more than just a current buzzword, it was practically the new norm with respect to child-rearing, with the emphasis on meeting the needs of the child and nurturing his relationship with each parent.

Erin didn't think that should be too difficult for her and Kyle to manage. After all, they'd been friends for a long time and lovers for only one night.

One incredible, bliss-filled night the memory of which, more than eleven months later, still haunted her dreams.

"I don't know about this," Erin said, as she followed Kyle toward the front doors of Jo's Pizza. "Showing up here with the baby kind of feel likes an ambush."

"I invited her to come to my place this morning," he reminded her. "But she claimed that she had to be at the restaurant early to have a new oven installed."

"You don't think it's true?"

"I think she's always busy doing something," he hedged.

"We could wait until she's less busy," she suggested.

"I don't want to have to keep our baby hidden from the local gossips until she can fit us into her schedule."

A fair point, she acknowledged, but as Kyle slid his key in the lock, she still felt uneasy about what they were doing.

The bell over the door jingled when he pushed it open and ushered Erin inside.

"We're not open for lunch yet," Jo called out from the back. "Come back at eleven thirty."

Then her voice dropped to a lower volume as she demanded to know which of her employees had forgotten to relock the door after they arrived—all of whom denied culpability.

Kyle set Joel's car seat on top of the closest table. The baby looked up, always intrigued by new places—and totally fascinated by the wide blades of the ceiling fan that spun slowly overhead.

"We're not here for lunch," Kyle called back.

But the rich scents of tomato, garlic and oregano teased Erin's nostrils and her stomach rumbled.

"I could go for a slice of pizza," she said.

"Didn't you have breakfast?" Kyle asked, sounding both baffled and amused.

"Three hours ago," she said.

"Kyle?" Jo came out of the kitchen, drying her hands on a red-and-white checked tea towel. "What are you doing here?" Then her gaze shifted to the woman standing beside her son, and when she spoke again, her tone had softened. "Erin. I was so sorry to hear about your dad."

"Thank you," she said, her response muffled by the other woman's warm embrace. "The flowers you sent were really lovely."

"I just wanted you to know that I was thinking about you." Jo stepped back again then—and finally spotted the baby. "Oh my goodness…where did he come from?" She looked around, as if for errant parents who might have abandoned their infant in her restaurant.

"He came with us," Kyle told her.

"With you?" Jo stepped closer to peek at the baby, and Joel offered her a gummy smile. She glanced over her shoulder at Erin. "He's yours?"

She nodded, a tremulous smile curving her lips.

"And mine," Kyle said. "Which makes him your grandson."

"Oh. Oh my goodness," Jo said again, sinking into the nearest chair. "I'm going to need a minute."

She spent that minute looking at the baby through eyes blurred with tears. "Hey, there," she crooned, gently rubbing his cheek with the back of a finger. "I'm your Grandma Jo."

Joel kicked his legs, another smile curving his lips.

"I have so many questions," Jo said. "But the most pressing one right now is—can I hold him?"

"Of course," Erin said.

Jo didn't wait for assistance but immediately reached to unbuckle the harness and lift the baby out of the carrier to cuddle him close.

"See?" Kyle whispered to Erin. "Magic."

But she wasn't convinced—or the least bit surprised when Jo said, "I'm going to need an explanation."

"The short version is that I was so caught up in everything going on with my dad that I didn't think about the repercussions of keeping the news of my pregnancy to myself," Erin said, fully prepared to take all blame for the situation, because it was her fault.

"No one can deny that it must have been a difficult time for you," Jo said. "But we might have been able to make it a little easier, if we'd known everything that was happening."

"I'm sorry," Erin said sincerely, lowering herself into the chair across from her son's grandmother.

"I don't need an apology," Jo said. "How can I be mad when I've finally got a grandbaby to hold?"

"Not just a grandbaby," Kyle told her. "But a namesake of sorts. Grandma Jo, meet Joel Brian Landry."

"Oh, I like that," Jo said, her eyes shimmering again. "I like that a lot." Then she chuckled. "Your sister's going to be annoyed, though. Thrilled to meet her nephew, of course, but annoyed that her baby won't be the first grandbaby." She smiled as she shook her head. "Everything always was a competition between the two of you."

"And I win this round, right?" Kyle said.

Before his mom could respond—or maybe she chose not to indulge his childish behavior with a response—Kyle's phone chimed.

He pulled it out of his pocket, frowning as read the message on the screen. "I have to run over to The Home Station," he said. "Rizwan thinks the supplier sent cremini mushrooms instead of the shiitake that I ordered."

"He doesn't know for sure?"

"Apparently not," Kyle said. "And that would be why he still gets all the grunt jobs in the kitchen."

"I guess that's our cue to say goodbye," Erin said, pushing her chair away from the table.

"You said you wanted pizza," Jo reminded her, clearly unwilling to hand over her newly discovered grandbaby just yet.

"It's been a long time since I've had your pizza," Erin said. "But Kyle's obviously anxious to sort out his fungi problem and he's our ride."

"If you want to stay for lunch, I can swing by to pick you up later," he said, no doubt so that his mom could enjoy some more time with her grandson—and score bonus points for him.

"I would love to," Erin agreed. "I've been craving a slice with sausage and roasted red peppers since we walked through the door."

"If it doesn't take too long to sort out the mushroom issue, I'll come back and share your pizza."

"I'm really hungry," she warned. "Maybe I won't want to share."

"Order a large," he suggested. "If I don't make it back, you'll have leftovers for lunch tomorrow."

"I guess I'm ordering a large," Erin said to Jo.

"I'll get Frank right on that," Jo promised, already heading to the kitchen.

With the baby still in her arms.

"She's never going to give him back, is she?" Erin asked.

Kyle chuckled. "She won't have any choice when he gets hungry—or when her customers do."

When he'd gone, Jo returned with the baby and a big glass of water for Erin. "I know you like Coke, but all the chemicals in that stuff can't be good for a baby."

"I gave up soda—and coffee—when I found out I was pregnant."

Jo nodded briskly. "Good girl."

"Tired girl," Erin said. "You wouldn't believe how much I miss my morning hit of caffeine."

"I would believe it," Jo assured her. "I gave it up, too, when I was expecting both Kyle and Lucy, substituting peppermint tea instead."

"That's been my go-to," she said, as Frank came out of the kitchen with a stack of plates and napkins in his hands.

"I get paid to cook, not serve." Despite his grumbling tone, he winked at Erin as he set the items on the table.

"I wouldn't pay you to serve," Jo told him. "Your pizza crust might be legendary, but your customer service sucks."

"Pizza smells great, Frank," Erin told him.

"You can tell me it tastes great in another two minutes."

"I will," she promised.

"Good to see you around here again."

She smiled. "It's good to be here again."

He inclined his head toward the baby on Jo's lap. "Cute kid. Yours?"

She nodded.

"Feel free to bring him around here anytime."

"I didn't know you liked babies," Jo said to her cook.

"I like this one," he said. "Because he keeps you out of my kitchen."

And with that, he retreated to it again.

Jo shook her head. "I swear that man gets more ornery every day."

"But his pizza crust *is* legendary," Erin reminded her.

"Without sauce, pizza crust is nothing more than flatbread," Jo said pointedly, when Frank returned with a tray of pizza.

"Without crust, pizza sauce is just sad," he retorted.

Erin couldn't help but smile as she listened to their exchange. "I think I missed listening to the two of you bicker as much as I missed Jo's pizza."

"Didn't Lucy send pizza to you when you were

in Arkansas?" Jo asked, as Erin transferred a slice from the pan to her plate.

"Not enough," she said. "Especially considering that my family made me share."

Jo chuckled at that, and Joel tipped his head back to look at her.

"None for you just yet," she said to the infant. "But I promise, when you've got the teeth to chew it, Grandma Jo will give you all the pizza you want."

"And who knows?" Erin said. "Maybe he'll be such a big fan that he wants to work with his grandma at Jo's Pizza someday."

"Or he might follow in his dad's footsteps," Jo said. "Or his mom's."

"Whatever he wants to do or be when he grows up, he'll be loved and supported," Erin promised.

"I haven't been very supportive of Kyle, have I?" Though Jo was obviously talking to Erin now, she kept her attention on the baby.

"I wasn't trying to make a statement about your relationship with your son," she assured her baby's grandmother.

"You don't need to," Jo said. "I'm all too aware of the distance in my relationship with Kyle. A distance that I allowed to grow."

"I'm hardly an expert on parent-child relationships," Erin said. "But, brother-in-law, who is a civil engineer, is fond of saying that there's no distance so great that it cannot be spanned by a bridge, provided the foundation is solid enough."

"I'll keep that in mind," Jo promised.

Chapter Twelve

The day after the outing to Jo's Pizza, Erin sat with her phone in hand, desperately wanting to reach out to Lucy. Her friend's contact information was displayed on the screen—she just needed to gather the courage to connect the call——but she wasn't sure what to say after keeping a secret so big for so long.

Before she could figure out the answer to that question, a knock sounded, and opening the door, she found herself face-to-face with her best friend.

"Ohmygod—look at you," Erin said, her eyes filling with tears as she greeted her very pregnant friend. "You are totally glowing."

"I'm sweating," Lucy corrected. "Because growing a baby has thrown my internal thermostat out of whack. But I don't care that I'm sweating, I'm going to hug you anyway because I've missed you like crazy."

Erin laughed as she returned her friend's embrace. "I've missed you, too. And your whacked-out thermostat notwithstanding, you look absolutely fabulous."

"I feel pretty good—other than the occasional flare-up of sciatica when the baby puts pressure on the nerve." Her expression turned serious as she took Erin's hands. "I'm so sorry I couldn't be with you for your dad's funeral."

"It's okay," Erin said. "You had the very best reason not to be there. Although, a heads-up that your brother was coming might have been good."

"I didn't think you'd be surprised to see him." She met her friend's gaze squarely. "Of course, I didn't know you'd had his child, either, so obviously we need to work on our communication skills."

"It's been an eventful eleven-and-a-half months," Erin told her, hedging.

"We've got a lot to catch up on," Lucy agreed. "But first, I want to meet my nephew."

"Apparently he wants to meet you, too," she said, as a soft cooing emanated from the baby monitor on the counter.

"Oh." Lucy pressed a hand to her heart. "Those cute little baby sounds just make me go all soft and gooey inside."

"He makes other sounds, too, that aren't nearly as cute," Erin told her, leading the way to the baby's room. "Especially at three o'clock in the morning."

"I don't believe it," her friend said, reaching into the crib to pick up the baby. "Hey, there, sweetie. It's your Auntie Lucy. I'm so happy to finally meet you."

Joel, always happy to be the center of attention, responded with a happy smile.

"Oh." Lucy's eyes got misty. "Look at that—is he really smiling at me?"

"He's really smiling at you," Erin confirmed.

"You have no idea how much I wanted to camp out on your doorstep, waiting for you to come home, so I could meet him. The only thing that held me back was knowing that my mother would never forgive me if I got to see him first."

"I guess she told you that we were at the pizzeria yesterday?" Erin said.

"She told me. Frank told me. Mrs. Eldridge who comes in for lunch every Friday told me. And Tom Gilchrist from the hardware store told me."

"I almost forgot that the Haven rumor mill is a well-oiled piece of machinery," Erin said. "And still, I missed this town and everyone in it."

"Which is why you're never allowed to leave Haven for anything more than a long weekend again."

Erin laughed, even as her eyes filled with tears. "Of course, I missed you most of all."

"Don't think that's going to let you off the hook for never telling me that you were pregnant," Lucy said, sounding hurt. "I thought I was your best friend."

"You are," Erin assured her. "You have no idea

how much I wanted to tell you, how hard it was to not to say something every time we talked on the phone. How hard it was not to call you when I had my first ultrasound, when I felt the first flutter of movement and when my water broke—at midnight."

"So why didn't you?" Lucy wanted to know.

"Because how could I admit that I'd gotten pregnant after one night when you and Claudio had been trying for so long to have a child?"

"When you put it that way, I guess I can understand why you held back," her friend acknowledged.

"Plus, you would have had all kinds of questions about the father."

"I still do," her friend said. "I mean, I know it's Kyle—but knowing that…thinking about you and my brother…together…it makes my head spin and raises a million more questions."

"It wasn't something either of us planned," Erin told her.

"I don't need the details," Lucy assured her. "But I wish you'd told me. And yeah, maybe it would have taken me some time to be okay with the fact that you were having a baby before me—when I wasn't sure if I'd ever be able to get pregnant—but I would have been there for you."

"I know, there was just so much happening all at once."

"I can't imagine how hard it must have been to go through everything on your own. And at the same time that you were dealing with your dad's illness."

"I wasn't really on my own," Erin said.

"Do you have another best friend in Silver Hook that you haven't told me about?"

"Of course not. I was actually referring to my sister."

"Anna?"

She nodded. "Yeah, it was a surprise to me, too. But she was incredible. Maybe it was because she got pregnant first, so she got to play big sister for a change, but she was helpful and supportive."

"I'm glad," Lucy said sincerely. "But I'm even more glad that you're home now, where you belong."

While Erin was visiting with Lucy, Kyle was in his tiny office at The Home Station, putting the finishing touches on the "Daily Specials" menu insert for the day. He'd just clicked Print when a knock sounded on the open door.

He glanced up to see his boss standing there.

"Are we all booked up for tonight?" Liam Gilmore asked.

"It's Saturday," Kyle told him, as if the answer should be just as obvious.

"Any chance you can squeeze in another table for two at eight o'clock?"

Of course, Kyle knew that when Liam asked if there was any chance, he was really telling the chef to make it happen.

"Special occasion?"

His boss nodded. "There's a young couple staying in The Wild Bill Suite this weekend. He was planning to propose over a candlelight dinner, but he forgot to book the dining room when he booked the suite."

Kyle looked at the reservation book. "It will be really tight," he warned. "A preferable option might be room service. We can set up a table in the alcove by the window. Linen tablecloth and napkins, flowers and candles."

"That sounds like an even better idea," Liam agreed. "With the added bonus of privacy to celebrate their engagement after he puts the ring on her finger."

"Or a lack of witnesses to his humiliation if she turns him down," Kyle countered.

"Who would have guessed that a man who puts so much of his heart and soul into his cooking would have a cynical streak?" his boss mused.

"It's not cynicism, it's realism. When a man asks the ultimate yes-or-no question, he should be prepared for the possibility that he could hear either answer."

"Let me guess—Erin turned you down?"

Because, of course, his boss knew, along with everyone else in town, that Erin's baby was his baby, too. Less than forty-eight hours after her return, the local gossip proved once again to be even hotter than the coffee at The Daily Grind.

"I haven't asked her to marry me," he said, demonstrating that his boss didn't know everything.

"Why not?" Liam asked.

"Because I didn't imagine myself ever going down that path," Kyle confided.

"You care about Erin, don't you?"

"Of course."

"And she cares about you?"

"Yes."

"And you want to be there for your son?" his boss pressed.

"More than anything," he admitted.

"Then you should want to marry his mom," Liam said.

Kyle was afraid it might be as simple—and as complicated—as that.

The last few diners were lingering over dessert and coffee when word came down to the kitchen from The Wild Bill Suite that the yes-or-no question had been answered with an enthusiastic "yes," putting the staff in a celebratory mood as they cleaned up.

"Customers aren't allowed in the kitchen," Kyle admonished, when Lucy walked in.

"I'm not a customer, I'm your sister."

"You still shouldn't be back here. And what are you doing here so late, anyway?" he asked, more curious than concerned.

"I wanted cheesecake," she admitted.

"You know you can get cheesecake from Sweet Caroline's, which is, in fact, where we get our desserts," he reminded her.

"Okay, I wanted cheesecake *and* I wanted to talk to you."

"So talk," he told her.

"I'm waiting for my cheesecake."

He sighed. "Chocolate sauce or fresh strawberry topping?"

"Mmm...both?"

"That's not actually an option," he told her.

She smiled sweetly.

"Except for my sister, apparently."

He gestured to Rizwan, who, despite his lack of knowledge of fungi, had a nice touch with desserts. "I need a slice of cheesecake with chocolate sauce and strawberry topping."

"Yes, chef," the line cook said, and hurried away to prep the dish.

Lucy smiled warmly at the man when he returned with a square plate elaborately decorated with swirls of chocolate and strawberry coulis on top of which sat a thick wedge of cheesecake covered in strawberries and chocolate sauce and mounds of whipped cream. "Thank you, Rizwan."

The line cook nodded and ducked away again.

"Can you talk now?" Kyle asked.

"It would be easier for me to eat this if I was sitting down," Lucy said.

He gestured to his office.

Of course, the visitor's chair was covered in catalogues and samples, so Lucy took the chair behind his desk.

His chair.

He folded his arms over his chest and leaned back against the filing cabinet, giving his sister *the look* that would have sent any of his kitchen staff scrambling.

Lucy ignored him.

"I saw Erin today—and finally met my nephew," she said, as she dipped her fork into the cake. "You made a cute kid, big brother."

"Yeah, he's pretty great."

"And you and Erin?" she prompted. "How are you guys?"

"We've got some things to figure out."

She nodded. "That's understandable."

"I'm still mad at her," Kyle admitted. "Or I want to be. Then I remember how it felt the very first time I held the baby—*my son*—in my arms, and suddenly the hurt and anger aren't nearly as strong as all these other emotions."

"I love to hear you say '*my son*,'" Lucy marveled, a smile curving her lips. "I still can hardly believe that my big brother's a daddy."

"Yeah." He scrubbed his hands over his face. "I can hardly believe it some days, too."

"Although, it was almost a bigger surprise for me to find out that you'd hooked up with Erin. I'm still trying wrap my head around the idea of the two of you together—I don't mean that I'm thinking of you *together together*, because…no. Not going there. But you and Erin… I think I'm okay with that. In fact, I love the idea of my best friend being my sister-in-law—"

"Whoa!" He held up a hand. "I think you're jumping the gun a little bit there."

She frowned as she lifted another forkful of cheesecake to her lips. "Are you telling me that you haven't already proposed to her?"

"I only found out about the baby last week," he reminded her.

"And as soon as you realized that her baby was your baby, you should have asked her to marry you."

"It's the twenty-first century. Aren't we past the point where a man and woman have to get married because they have a child together?"

"Sure," she agreed. "If the mother of your child was some anonymous woman that you only spent one night with, I wouldn't be suggesting that you put a ring on her finger. But this is *Erin*."

"With whom I only spent one night."

"Oh, I see," she said, a definite edge in her tone. "You got what you wanted and that was the end of it?"

"It was what we both wanted."

"But that wasn't the end of it, was it? Because you have real feelings for Erin. That's why you were out of sorts the whole time that she was away."

"I wasn't out of sorts," he denied. "I was worried about her, because I know how close she was to her dad and how devastated she was by his diagnosis."

"And you missed her."

"Well, yeah," he admitted. "We used to spend a lot of time together because we were friends and neighbors and coworkers."

"And lovers."

"For one night," he said again. "Don't try to make it into something more than that."

She pointed her fork at him. "You spent one night with a woman you like and respect and with whom you now have a child. Don't try to make it into less."

Despite the hurtful words that Bonnie had spoken to her daughter the day after the funeral, Erin had been in regular contact with her mom since her return to Haven. Though she'd long ago accepted that they would never be close like Bonnie and Anna were close, Erin had an obvious and deep affection for her mom, and she worried about her.

As Mother's Day approached, she worried even more because Brian had always made a big fuss over his wife—the mother of his children—and there wouldn't be a big fuss this year. Yet one more reminder to Bonnie that her life had irrevocably changed seven weeks earlier.

But Erin sent flowers, and made the requisite phone call. They didn't talk long, because Ian and Marissa and the girls were there to visit, which was good news to Erin, who was a lot less worried when she ended the call.

She was so focused on it being her mom's first Mother's Day without her husband that Erin might have forgotten it was her own first Mother's Day, if not for the beautiful bouquet of flowers delivered by Blossom's Flower Shop, with a card signed "Love, Joel."

Of course, she knew that Kyle had actually sent

the flowers, and she chose to interpret the gesture as a sign that he was no longer mad at her—or at least not holding a grudge. Over the past few weeks, they'd both been trying to focus on the present rather than the past, and she would say they'd made definite progress in their efforts to co-parent, giving her hope that they might learn to be friends again, too.

She was thrilled with the flowers, but Kyle didn't stop there. After Mother's Day Brunch—one of the busiest days of the year at The Home Station—he showed up at Erin's apartment with a box of food and equipment to cook for her before he had to go back to the restaurant again for the dinner shift.

Not only did he cook, he made her favorite: Belgian waffles with strawberry topping and whipped cream. The waffles were served with a side of perfectly browned sausage links and a crystal flute filled with freshly squeezed orange juice and just a splash of champagne.

And then, when she'd cleaned her plate, he took it away and gave her a small box wrapped in gold paper. Inside the box was a heart-shaped locket, and inside the locket was a tiny picture of Joel, and she was helpless to hold back the tears that spilled onto her cheeks as he fastened the chain around her throat.

"If you want to exchange it for something else, I can take it back," he said, deliberately misinterpreting the reason for her tears.

She clutched the locket. "Don't you dare."

He chuckled at that.

"Thank you. Sincerely," she said. "You've made my first Mother's Day truly special."

"Thank you for being an amazing mom to our son."

The sincerity in his tone made her eyes fill again.

There were no tissues around, so Kyle handed her a clean napkin, and she managed to smile through her tears.

"Are those waterworks going to turn off anytime soon?"

"If you think this is bad, you should have seen me when I was pregnant."

But, of course, she hadn't given him that option—though he refrained from pointing that out to her.

"Will you tell me about it now?" he asked instead.

She nodded. "What do you want to know?"

"Why don't we start with when you realized you were pregnant," he suggested.

"Okay." She dabbed at her eyes, then crumpled the napkin into her fist. "It took me longer to figure out than it probably should have," she admitted. "That day in the cabin—you said that I had nine months to figure out how to tell you, but that isn't really true. I didn't know—or even suspect—until I was in my fifth month."

"How is that possible?" he asked. "I mean, I've heard about women who give birth and claim they didn't know they were pregnant, but I've always been skeptical of those stories."

"I don't think I could have gone another four months—or even four weeks—without figuring things out, especially once my belly started to grow," Erin told him, lifting the fussy baby from his chair to settle him at her breast. "But for the first several months, I was so preoccupied with my dad and his treatments and helping out at the resort that I wasn't paying attention to what was happening with my own body.

"I think I realized, fairly early on, that I'd skipped a period or two, but stress has always affected my cycle. And I didn't have any nausea or other telltale symptoms, and the possibility of a pregnancy never crossed my mind because we'd taken precautions."

"What finally clued you in?"

"Anna," she confided, easing the baby from her breast to burp him. "We usually did the weekly grocery shopping together, and one day, as we were making our way up and down the aisles, we saw that the Halloween candy was out—despite the fact that it was early September. And I suddenly had an intense craving for peanut butter cups, so I threw a big bag in the cart, and the next week, I bought another bag—having polished off the first one entirely by myself—and she jokingly remarked that maybe I was pregnant.

"Of course, I dismissed the possibility. How could I be pregnant when I hadn't had sex in five months? But then I remembered the missed periods and I started to panic, wondering if I could possibly be five months pregnant.

"The next day, Anna picked up a test from the pharmacy, and when I finally got up the nerve to take it, the result was an unmistakable plus sign in the little window." She looked at Kyle then, hoping to make him understand the emotional turmoil she'd felt in that moment. "I wanted to tell you. I desperately wanted to tell you. But as I sat there, staring at the stick and marveling over the fact that I was going to have a baby—your baby—I couldn't forget that you'd told me, more than once, that you never wanted to be a father."

"You know why I said that. And that what I really meant was that I never wanted to be like *my* father."

"I do," she agreed. "And I was pretty sure that, despite the feelings you'd professed, you'd be a wonderful father to our child."

"So why didn't you tell me?" he asked her again.

"Because I wasn't one hundred percent sure. Because there was a tiny part of me that was afraid you wouldn't want our baby."

And she didn't want to subject Joel to that kind of rejection. The same kind of parental rejection that had scarred each of his parents.

And maybe she was afraid that, despite their long-standing friendship, he'd reject her, too.

"I hate knowing that you had even a smidgen of doubt," he said.

"I don't anymore," she told him, rising to her feet with the baby.

"Good." He nodded and followed her to the nursery. "Because I'm going to be here—for Joel and for you. Whatever you need."

"And you went above and beyond today," she said, as they tiptoed out of the baby's room. "Thank you."

"Happy first Mother's Day," he said, and touched his lips to hers.

It obviously wasn't the first time he'd kissed her, but it was the first time in a very long time, and though she suspected he hadn't intended it to be more than a casual brush of his lips over hers, the moment their mouths touched, everything changed.

She'd started to think that the chemistry between them was a thing of the past. That whatever connection they'd once shared had been obliterated by her secrets and lies. Apparently she'd been wrong.

He cupped her head, tipping it back so that he could deepen the kiss. His scent—that familiar and surprisingly seductive combination of basil and lime—teased her senses. His hands—those strong and oh-so-talented hands—tempted her body.

They'd been down this road before, she reminded herself, summoning the memory as a warning. Instead it had the opposite effect, heightening her awareness and intensifying her desire.

She lifted her arms to link them around his neck and pressed her body closer to his, so that they were connected mouth to mouth, thigh to thigh, and generating all kinds of heat in between. It was so much more than a kiss—it was a total sensual assault. And when his tongue slid between her lips, she met it with her own.

Since the night they'd spent together, she'd almost managed to convince herself that the experience couldn't possibly have been as amazing as she remembered. That her overactive imagination combined with an overload of baby hormones running rampant through her system had made it into something more.

Kissing him now, Erin realized she'd been wrong.

Kissing him now, she was forced to acknowledge that her memory had failed her, that her recollection of kissing Kyle paled in comparison to the reality.

Only when they were both out of breath did he ease his mouth from hers. After she'd managed to pull air into her lungs and clear some of the lust that clouded her brain, she pulled out of his arms to put some much-needed space between them.

"That was...um..."

"Um-mazing?" he suggested.

She pressed her lips together, as if that might stop them from tingling. But it wasn't just her lips that were tingling. She could feel the effects of his kiss all the way to her toes.

And yes, "amazing" was definitely one word for it. But she had another one.

"It was a mistake," she said.

"I don't think so," he said. "And I don't believe you do, either."

"What I think is that our relationship is already complicated enough without adding...chemistry... to the mix."

"If the chemistry wasn't already there, we wouldn't have Joel," he pointed out.

A valid point, she acknowledged, if only to herself.

* * *

Maybe Erin was right to resist the attraction between them, Kyle considered when he was back in his own apartment later that night.

The first few days that she'd been home had been a little awkward as they'd tried to figure out this co-parenting thing that she was so keen on—and he tried to remember that he was furious with her for keeping her pregnancy and then the birth of their child a secret. Then he'd look at that child—their son—and be filled with such a powerful rush of love, it pushed aside all other emotions, making it impossible for him to stay mad.

But maybe it would be a mistake to risk the tentative truce they'd established in recent weeks for the possibility that they might build something more.

Or maybe his sister had a point. Maybe things would be much simpler all around if he and Erin were married. Certainly they wouldn't need to debate the pros and cons of giving in to the physical attraction between them if they were husband and wife. He could go to sleep beside her every night, wake up next to her every morning and make love with her whenever they wanted—an idea that held definite appeal. Not a reason to get married, but a definite perk.

The abysmal failure of his parents' marriage had led him to conclude that he wasn't a candidate for wedded bliss. Despite the societal pressure that made most people believe marriage was a normal rite of passage, Kyle had never aspired to fall in love, get married and eventually have a couple of kids. And a string of failed relationships had only strengthened his determination to remain single.

But now he was a dad—and that changed everything. It was no longer about what he wanted for his life but what was best for his son—and that was the stability and security of a family.

Now Kyle just had to convince Erin of that fact.

Chapter Thirteen

Erin was both excited and a little apprehensive as she waited for Kyle to show up Monday morning for The Big Event.

Okay, maybe it wasn't a capital-letter-worthy big event, but it was a significant milestone for their son—his first day having solid food.

"I don't know whose definition of solid this is," Erin remarked, stirring the rice cereal she'd prepared in accordance with the directions on the box. "But Dr. Tahir says this is what we start with."

Joel's gaze was locked on the spoon, as if he somehow knew that the cereal was for him. Or maybe he just liked the red spoon and matching bowl.

At precisely 8:00 a.m., there was a knock on the door.

"It's open."

Kyle walked in, nodding as he wished her a "good morning" before greeting his son with a bright smile. "Hey, there, big guy."

Joel smiled back as his dad settled into the chair beside him.

Erin handed Kyle the bowl.

"You want me to do this?" he asked, sounding surprised.

"Don't you want to do it?"

"I don't know what I'm doing," he warned.

"Then it'll be the first time for both of you."

Kyle picked up the spoon and dipped it into the cereal. "This is solid food?"

She laughed as she opened the camera app on her phone, determined to capture the milestone moment for posterity. "According to the doctor."

"Okay, here we go," he said, lifting the spoon out of the bowl and moving it toward the baby's mouth.

Joel instinctively opened up, allowing his dad to feed him.

"Look at that," Kyle remarked proudly.

Erin was looking—and recording everything.

Including when Joel decided to push his tongue out of his mouth, dribbling most of the cereal down his chin.

"*Don't* look at that," Kyle said now, making Erin laugh again.

He lifted the bottom of the baby's bib to wipe his chin. Then he spooned up some more cereal to try again, and again Joel spit it out.

"Maybe he doesn't like it."

"If he didn't like it, he wouldn't keep opening his mouth," Erin pointed out.

"But he keeps spitting it out."

"Probably just a reflex," she said. "He'll figure it out."

"I guess we've both got a lot to learn," Kyle said, speaking to his son now.

Joel responded by opening his mouth, a wordless plea for more.

"That was an experience," Kyle said, when the cereal bowl was finally empty—more of it likely on the baby's bib than in his tummy.

"And tomorrow morning you get to do it again— if you want," Erin hastened to clarify.

He nodded. "I'll be here."

She wiped Joel's face and hands, then lifted him out of his highchair. Kyle rose to his feet, too, and she was suddenly aware that she was as close to him now as she'd been when he kissed her the day before. And for a brief moment, when his gaze dropped to her mouth, she thought he might also be remembering that kiss.

But then, totally out of the blue, he said, "I think we should get married."

She paused, waiting for the punch line, certain that he was joking.

"You're serious," she realized, when no follow-up came.

"Of course, I'm serious," he said. "I've been doing a lot of thinking and getting married makes sense."

"Well, what woman wouldn't get all fluttery over such a romantic proposal?" she said, irritated with herself because there wasn't anything at all romantic about his proposal, and yet she was feeling fluttery inside.

"Do you want romance?" he asked. "Flowers? Candlelight?"

"I want you to tell me where this is coming from."

"I don't want to have to knock on the door in the morning to see my son, or go home after tucking him into bed at night. I want to be there for everything—to help not just with cereal in the morning but feedings in the middle of the night and everything in between."

"I know you're thinking about what is best for Joel, but in all the years I've known you, I've never before heard you express any interest in getting married."

"Maybe I wasn't ready for anything more when I dated those other women."

"And now you're ready?" She couldn't help but sound skeptical.

"I think I might be."

"You'll forgive me if I don't get all tongue-tied over 'maybes' and 'might bes.'"

"What do you want me to say? What are the magic words you need to hear to give us a chance? Because making this relationship work matters to me. Because you and Joel matter to me.

"I know I don't have any experience with successful relationships—or any particularly good role models, either—but I promise, if you give me a chance, I will do everything in my power to make our relationship work, to be the best husband that I can be to you and the best father that I can be to Joel."

She knew he was speaking from the heart. His tone was both earnest and raw as he laid his soul bare. But he didn't love her, and she'd spent too many years feeling unlovable and unloved to settle for a loveless marriage.

"You're already a great dad," she said, and meant it.

"I still struggle with diaper changes," he acknowledged ruefully.

"It wasn't so long ago that you didn't know which part of a diaper was front and which was back," she reminded him. "But you showed an interest, you asked questions and you made the effort."

"I also made some mistakes—and no doubt, I'm going to make a lot more," he said. "But hopefully none that will do any lasting damage."

"I make mistakes, too," she told him. "You should have seen me the first few weeks as I struggled to nurse him."

"I wish I had," he said softly.

She winced.

He touched a hand to her arm. "I didn't say that to make you feel bad—only to let you know that I sincerely wish I'd been there for you, so that I could have struggled along with you."

"But I do feel bad," she said. "I didn't mean to deprive you of those first weeks with your son."

"I know," Kyle said, because it was true.

Another truth was that, even if he'd known about Joel, he couldn't have been in Silver Hook with Erin and their son because he had responsibilities here. He was the executive chef of The Home Station—his name was etched in the glass on the door. After years of toiling away in other people's kitchens, he was finally in charge of his own.

A wife and kids hadn't been anywhere on his radar. And he couldn't have guessed how much it would mean to him to be a father until the very first time he'd held his son in his arms. In that moment, he'd known that there wasn't anything he wouldn't do for his child. And one of the things he really wanted for his child was a family.

"Tell me about those first weeks," he urged.

"You want to know how badly I screwed up?" she guessed. "That I couldn't figure out how to get him to latch on properly, so he wasn't getting enough milk. Then, to make up for it, he was nursing almost constantly, so my nipples started to crack and bleed. And that's probably more information than you wanted."

He shook his head. "I want to know everything I missed. But mostly, I want to know that you're okay now."

"I'm okay," she assured him.

"I couldn't be there to help you then," he noted. "But I want to be here to help you now."

"You are here."

"I don't mean right now but always," he clarified.

"As your husband and a father to our son—and any other children we might have in the future."

"We can co-parent without being married. In fact, that's what we've been doing, and quite successfully, for the past several weeks."

"I don't want to co-parent," he insisted stubbornly. "I want us to be a family."

"We're not getting married," she said, matching his tone.

"I want to be here for Joel. For him and for you."

"I will do everything I can to accommodate your relationship with our son, but I can't marry you. I can't stand before a minister—or even a justice of the peace—and exchange vows that we wouldn't keep."

"I would keep them," he assured her. "I do honor and cherish you."

"But you don't love me," she said.

"I care about you."

"And I care about you, too much to screw everything up by saying yes to a marriage proposal you blurted out because you believe that getting married is the right thing to do."

It might have been easy for Erin to dismiss Kyle's impulsive proposal, but it wasn't so easy for her to forget it. Saying no had been the right thing to do, but she couldn't deny that she'd been tempted—if only for a moment—to say yes. Not only because she wanted to give their son a family, but because at some point over the past few weeks—or maybe during the previous seven years—she'd realized that she was falling in love with Kyle.

At least, she was pretty sure that what she was feeling was love. But the truth was, her emotions had been running high for months, forcing her to consider the possibility that what she felt wasn't love for Kyle but an overflow of the emotion that connected her to their son. Except that the more time she spent with Kyle and Joel, the deeper she fell in love with both of them.

So maybe she could imagine herself someday reciting the traditional wedding vows to Kyle, but only if she believed that he loved her, too. Because marriage was a sacred institution not to be entered into casually or impulsively but only by two people who were in love and fully committed to one another.

Marrying Kyle because they both loved Joel would be wrong for so many reasons.

But she couldn't deny that she would be tempted to say yes, if only she could believe that he might someday love her, too.

Erin was looking forward to the meeting she'd scheduled for Tuesday morning with Quinn. Not only because she hadn't seen her friend since their arduous road trip, but also because it was a business meeting, which meant that she got to put on grown-up clothes and have a conversation with someone who was capable of talking back.

Of course, no one had told Erin that she had to live in leggings and flannel shirts when she was at home, but the stretchy pants were comfortable and the button-front shirts allowed quick access to her breasts at feeding time. And while she was hardly starved for conversation, considering that Kyle stopped by every day and often more than once a day, her routines were starting to feel a little stale and she was eager to shake them up a little.

She also believed that it was important for her to have her own life and career outside of being a mom, and she was fortunate that Kyle wasn't just willing but able to share the responsibilities of parenting. And if she was surprised that his schedule proved to be much more accommodating than she'd previously imagined, she was also grateful.

But as much as she'd been looking forward to her meeting, when she was finally ready to go, she discovered that she wasn't so eager to leave her baby.

"Are you sure you want to do this?" she asked Kyle, not wanting to admit that she was the one suddenly experiencing doubts. "Quinn probably wouldn't mind if I brought Joel with me."

"I'm thinking you don't trust me to do this," he said.

"Of course, I trust you," she hastened to assure him. Because she did. She knew Kyle loved their son and would take good care of him, but she'd never been away from Joel for more than an hour—and that was only to go to the grocery store. "I just think Quinn might be disappointed if I show up alone."

"If she is, you can show her the hundreds of photos and videos you have on your phone," he suggested.

She didn't argue the number. No doubt there were

hundreds—possibly even thousands—of pictures on her phone, because she always had it in hand to snap and share photos.

"Okay," she relented. "I'm going." She scooped the baby out of his seat to give him a last, quick cuddle. "You be a good boy for Daddy, okay?"

Joel gave her a gummy smile.

"I'll take that as a *yes*," she said, then brushed a kiss on the baby's cheek.

"What about me?" Kyle asked.

Though she rolled her eyes, she kissed his cheek, too, as she handed him the baby, and walked out of the apartment with her lips tingling.

Chapter Fourteen

As Erin drove to Cooper's Corners, she couldn't help but marvel over how much her life had changed in the past eight weeks since she'd returned to Haven.

It felt really good to be back, to be living her own life again. And while she felt certain that being a mom to Joel was the most important job she would ever do, she knew it was also important that she not allow her life to revolve around her son. Her clients had been understanding while she'd worked remotely from Silver Hook, but now that she was back, it was reasonable that they'd expect more personal attention. And she was happy to give that personal attention, especially when the client was also a friend.

Quinn lived with her grandfather in a two-story stone-and-brick house on the outer edge of town. Her office was above the double car garage, accessible by both interior and exterior doors. The first time Erin had met with Quinn there, she'd remarked on the convenience of being able to roll out of bed and go to work in pajamas. But Quinn never did, insisting that leaving the house and entering through the outside door helped put her in the mindset of "going to the office" so that as soon as she sat down behind her desk, she was ready to get started.

Through her connection to Quinn, Erin had done work for a couple of other authors and discovered that they all had their quirks. One fueled herself through revisions with diet Cokes and Oreos, and another did a ritualistic cleansing of her workspace before she started each new project. As long as their routines—and Erin—worked for them, she wasn't going to judge.

She pulled into the driveway, parking beside the Bookmobile that her friend drove around town every week, because apparently being a bestselling novelist didn't keep Quinn busy enough! As she climbed out of her car, she spotted Quinn's grandfather sitting on the porch, drinking his coffee and scrolling through the news on his iPad. Old Mr. Ellison, as he was referred to around town, had resisted technology for a long time, insisting that the only way to read a newspaper was in paper form—a conviction that had been tossed aside like yesterday's news when the *Herald*, Haven's local paper, went digital-only.

Erin lifted a hand in a wave as she made her way

to the side door and the stairs leading up to Quinn's office, and the old man returned the gesture.

"You're just on time," Quinn said, as the kettle started to whistle when Erin walked through the door.

"Are you making tea?" she asked, surprised because her friend was an avid coffee drinker.

"I figured that was your current preference, since you drank about ten gallons of it en route between Arkansas and Nevada."

"It is," Erin confirmed.

"I got cookies from Sweet Caroline's, too. Oatmeal chocolate chip and white chocolate macadamia nut."

"And I wonder why I'm still carrying seven pounds of baby fat," she lamented, even as she reached for a cookie from the plate on the table.

"Well, those seven pounds look good on you," her friend said, setting a mug of peppermint tea in front of Erin. "And another three would probably look even better."

"If you don't move this plate of cookies, I might add them," she warned.

Quinn chuckled as she took a seat across from her friend and helped herself to a cookie. "So...tell me how it's going."

"It's a struggle sometimes to squeeze work in during Joel's nap times," Erin said as she opened her laptop and keyed in her password. "But I think you're really going to like what—"

"I wasn't asking about the new website design,"

Quinn said, reaching across the table to gently close the computer again.

"Isn't that why I'm here?"

"Only partly," her friend said. "The bigger part—and what I was actually asking about—is how things are going with Kyle and the whole co-parenting arrangement."

"Oh. Um. Good. Things are good."

"You don't sound so sure about that," Quinn remarked.

"I'm not sure about anything anymore," she confided. "I thought things were good—and then he asked me to marry him."

"I'd take that as confirmation that things are going really well," her friend said.

"Except that he only asked me to marry him because he wants us to live and raise Joel together."

"And you want to marry for love," Quinn guessed.

"Is that too much to ask?"

"Of course not. I just think that people sometimes put too much stock in the words. Some guys will say 'I love you' at the drop of a hat—or in the hopes that they'll lead a woman to dropping her pants. Others don't say the words, but they show that they care in all the little and big things that they do."

Erin didn't disagree with what her friend was saying, but she worried that it was sometimes too easy to read into the little and big things so that they took on more significance than might have been intended. And when she thought about all the sweet and thoughtful things that Kyle had done for her over the past several weeks, she was afraid that she was seeing what she wanted to see and making a big deal out of nothing.

"Anyway, I told him *no* and that was that," she said. "Now tell me what's going on with you."

"My publisher wants me to do a book tour."

"That's not unusual," she remarked. "You've done one for each of your past six books."

"Yeah, and usually I'm happy to do them. The schedule is crazy, but it's fun to meet readers in different cities."

"So why aren't you happy about it this time?"

"Because of Steven," Quinn confided, naming the man she'd been dating for the past several months.

"You're afraid that you're going to miss him?" Erin guessed.

Her friend sighed and reached for another cookie. "Actually, I'm afraid that I won't."

"Oh."

"I hardly thought about him when I was in Silver Hook," Quinn confided now. "Of course, there was a lot of really interesting stuff going on there, so that might have had something to do with it.

"But if I do this book tour and don't miss him, then I'll have to break up with him when I get back, because what's the point of being in a relationship with someone who you don't even miss when you're apart? Other than to have a guaranteed date for holidays and family events, of course," she said, in answer to her own question.

"Is that really why you're with him?" Erin asked.

"So that you have someone to sit next to at Thanksgiving dinner or to dance with at a cousin's wedding?"

Quinn shrugged. "That and the sex is usually enjoyable."

"Usually enjoyable," she echoed dubiously, wondering why her amazing and talented friend would be willing to settle for mediocrity in any part of her life.

"He tries really hard," Quinn said, in defense of her boyfriend. "But it isn't always easy for me to shut off my brain and immerse myself in the moment."

"You shouldn't have to shut it off," Erin said. "When he kisses you, it should be with so much intensity and passion that you can't think about anything but how much you want him. And when you finally come together, you aren't just immersed in the moment—you *are* the moment, because everything outside of it ceases to exist, and even afterward, that single perfect moment lives on in your heart forever."

Quinn snatched up her notebook and pen from the table and frantically began scribbling. "Ohmygod, Erin—that's perfect. Absolute gold."

"Um…what's gold?" she asked, torn between bafflement and amusement as she watched her friend's pen fly over the page.

"What you just said. I've been struggling to write the love scene between Lily and Mark—I'm so much better at killing characters than the touchy-feely stuff—but what you just said now… I actually feel inspired."

"I'm…happy to help?" Erin said, sounding undecided.

Her friend laughed as she set the pen down and

snapped the cover of the book shut. "So tell me—
is that how you felt when you made love with Kyle?
Was it a single perfect moment that will live on in
your heart forever?"

"Why would you assume I was thinking of Kyle?"
she hedged. "Maybe I just read too many romance
novels."

"You can never read too much of anything,"
Quinn said. "Reading is to the mind what exercise
is to the body. And sex, if it's done right, is the very
best form of exercise. And it sounds to me like Kyle
does it right."

Erin sighed. "You're not going to let this go, are
you?"

"Having known each of you for a number of years,
I'm undeniably curious to know what caused the
chemistry between you to suddenly combust."

"The cause was a bottle of cabernet sauvignon,"
she said honestly.

"Hmm," Quinn said, clearly unconvinced. "Okay,
here's another question—for research purposes."

"Isn't everything for research purposes?"

"It's true I never know what might end up in one
of my books," her friend acknowledged. "But I always change names to protect the innocent."

"So what's your question?" Erin prompted.

"When you realized you were pregnant…were
you happy?" Quinn wondered.

"It took me a while to get to happy," she admitted.
"First there was shock, then panic, and then—when
I stopped thinking 'ohmygod, I'm pregnant' and

started to realize 'I'm going to have a baby'—such indescribable joy. I never even knew that I wanted a baby until I knew that I was pregnant."

"So maybe you won't know that you want a husband until you say yes to Kyle's proposal," her friend teased.

"It's not going to happen," Erin said firmly.

And for more reasons than she'd been willing to admit to Quinn—or even the man who'd asked her to marry him.

Life was pretty good, Kyle thought, as he dropped a pat of butter into the hot pan. It wasn't without challenges, but it was good. Of course, it would be even better when he finally convinced Erin to marry him so that they could live together with their son and be a real family, because he refused to give up on his conviction that it would happen.

He understood her reticence. He truly did. But her reticence was no match for his determination.

"Chef?"

"Hmm?"

"One of the guests at table four wants to speak to the you," Hanna said.

Kyle didn't look up. "Is there a problem with the food?" he asked, confident that there wasn't. Because nothing went out of his kitchen without being prepared and presented to his very exacting standards.

"I don't think so."

"Then whatever he wants can wait until I'm finished searing these salmon steaks."

She nodded, but instead of returning to the dining room to convey that information to the customer, she continued to hover.

"Was there something else, Hanna?"

"I think he might be someone you know—or at least someone who knows you," she explained. "Because he asked for you by name."

Which wasn't so unusual, considering that his name was not only on the frosted glass doors but printed on the menus.

But his curiosity was piqued now, and as soon as the salmon was plated with lemon butter broccolini and creamy risotto, he washed his hands and headed into the dining room, pivoting automatically toward table four.

He paused in midstride as he recognized the couple at the table: Martin Thomas and his wife, Amanda.

Kyle's father and stepmother.

He hadn't seen them in…two years?

Was that how long it had been since Fiona, his half sister, graduated from college? Kyle hadn't planned to attend the ceremony or the party afterward, but Fiona had pestered him for weeks and, in the end, he'd wanted to disappoint her even less than he'd wanted to avoid an altercation with Marty and Amanda.

He liked his half siblings well enough. He would willingly give up a kidney if Duncan, Callum or Fiona needed one, but that didn't mean he wanted to hang out with them. Every Easter, Thanksgiving and Christmas, he was invited to celebrate with his dad's second family. And every time, Kyle politely declined the invitation.

Because while Marty was busy with his second wife and their kids and her family, his first wife was on her own. Of course, Jo always insisted that it was her choice to be alone, and he didn't doubt that it was true. Even now, at fifty-eight years of age, she wasn't an unattractive woman. And on more than one occasion when he'd still been working at the pizzeria, he'd been a reluctant witness to male customers sniffing around his mom, interested in more than just her proprietary sauce recipe.

But Jo had never given any of them the time of day. No one aside from Niall Byrne. A lot of years earlier, Kyle had suspected there might be a romance blossoming between his mom and the banker who came in for lunch several times a month, but Jo had been quick to nip it in the bud. Though she seemed to enjoy Niall's flirtations, she didn't take them seriously. When Niall demanded to know why, she explained that he had to be younger than her by at least a decade—eleven years, it turned out—and to her mind, he couldn't possibly understand the obligations and responsibilities of a single mother. She made it clear that the restaurant and her kids were her priorities and the prospect of a romance wasn't going to crack the top ten.

Eventually Niall had given up and moved on, marrying Rhonda Barrow, an elementary school teacher, with whom he had two kids. A dozen years later,

Niall and Rhonda parted ways and now shared custody of their son and daughter and a goldendoodle named Ducky.

But according to Lucy, Niall had recently started coming around the restaurant again. And since Lucy and Claudio both worked at the pizzeria, they had a front-row seat to observe what was happening. With her daughter and son-in-law now partners in the business, Jo no longer had to be there from open to close, which meant that she actually had some free time. And apparently she was spending a lot of that time with Niall. They'd even been spotted sharing popcorn at Mann's Theater Saturday night, and Kyle was pretty sure the last time his mom had gone to the theater prior to that was when she took Lucy and him to see *Toy Story*.

So he was happy to know that Jo was finally starting to get on with her life, but that didn't make him any more inclined to forgive his father for his infidelity—or for leaving his first wife to struggle financially while he moved into a big, fancy house in Prospector Point that his second wife's father—one of Nevada's most successful builders—had gifted to them.

Amanda glanced up then and spotted him, lifting her hand to offer a tentative wave.

Having missed his opportunity to turn back around and retreat to the kitchen, Kyle continued on his way to the table.

"You're a long way from home, aren't you?" he asked, directing the question to his father.

"Friends of ours were here for brunch on Mother's Day and said it was more than worth the trip," Martin replied easily.

"Did you enjoy your prime rib?" he asked, noting that a small pool of au jus was the only remnant of the meal on his father's plate.

"It was incredibly tender and juicy."

Kyle directed the next question to his stepmother. "And how was your pasta primavera?"

"Delicious," she assured him.

"If you have room for dessert, I'd recommend the tiramisu cheesecake or the lemon sorbet with raspberry coulis."

"The sorbet sounds lovely," Amanda said.

"I'll send Hanna back to your table."

"Wait." Marty said. "Please."

"I really have to get back to the kitchen. I've got a dozen things going on that need my attention."

"We didn't just come here for dinner," his father said, as Kyle started to turn away. "We also wanted to invite you to our place next weekend. You and Erin and Joel."

He didn't need to ask how Marty knew about the baby—no doubt Lucy had filled him in on recent events. Perhaps it was because she'd been so young when their father walked out, and therefore less aware of the family's change in circumstances, that Lucy was more open to having a relationship with him now. Or maybe she was just a better person than Kyle. He suspected the truth might be a little bit of both, but either way, his sister had been in more regular contact with Marty in recent years than he'd done.

"Saturday or Sunday—your choice," Marty continued. "We can't promise a fancy meal like this, but we won't let you go hungry."

"I work the dinner shift on weekends," Kyle told him.

"Come early then. We'll have brunch."

"Or whenever you can," Amanda interjected. "You don't have to stay for a meal. Just come for a visit. Duncan, Callum and Fiona are as eager to meet their nephew as we are to meet our grandson."

And there it was—the frustratingly irrefutable fact that no matter how much he tried to limit his interactions with his father's second family, they were his family—which meant that they were Joel's family, too.

"I'll have to check with Erin and get back to you," he said, unwilling to commit.

Marty nodded. "We'll look forward to hearing from you."

It had been a brief and yet unsettling interaction, and Kyle hadn't quite succeeded in shaking off the mood when he left the restaurant at the end of his shift. He hated to think it was possible that he still resented his father for walking out on his family, because nearly a quarter century later, he should have gotten over it.

He didn't harbor any ill will toward his half siblings, but he wasn't sure he could say the same about his stepmother. Amanda claimed she didn't know

Marty was already married when she met him, and by the time she found out that he had a wife and child (and another one on the way!), it was too late. She was head over heels in love—and pregnant.

Kyle had spent a lot of years assuming that his father had been not just unfaithful but careless. Because it took less than half a minute to put on a condom before being intimate with a woman and anyone who couldn't be bothered to take that simple precaution deserved the consequences.

Of course, Kyle now knew that taking precautions wasn't always enough. That "ninety-eight percent effective" statistic was impressive, but the other two percent shouldn't to be ignored. Which made him wonder if his dad was a member of the exclusive two percent club, too, and maybe they had more in common than he realized.

Chapter Fifteen

Erin's brows lifted as she glanced at the clock when Kyle walked in while she was bathing their son in his baby tub, which was set carefully inside the big tub. "I wasn't expecting you for at least another hour."

He shrugged. "Service finished early, so I decided to take off and spend some extra time with Joel." He was already rolling back his sleeves to take over bath time duties, and Erin willingly stepped aside to let him.

After the baby was clean and dry and dressed in a sleeper with screen-printed images of the Golden Gate Bridge all over it—a souvenir from Uncle Owen and Uncle Roger's recent trip to San Francisco— Kyle sat down in the rocking chair with him to read a bedtime story, because Erin insisted that reading to him at a young age would provide the foundation for a lifetime habit. Of course, the book was all of ten pages, so five minutes later, he settled the now sleeping baby in his crib and ventured out to the living room where Erin was sitting cross-legged on the sofa, working on her laptop.

"I can't tell you how happy it makes me that you enjoy hanging out with Joel," she said, when he dropped into the chair facing her. "But he's only four months old. I don't think you need to adjust your schedule to accommodate his just yet."

"But if I don't start making changes now, I'll be working all the time when he's four years old, and by the time he's fourteen, I won't even know him."

Her gaze narrowed speculatively. "Did you talk to your dad today?"

"What? Where did that come from?"

"You're always a little on edge after he calls."

"Am I?" He frowned, uncomfortable with the realization that he wasn't as unaffected by his interactions with his father as he wanted to be.

"So he didn't call?" she pressed.

"No. But he and Amanda had dinner at the restaurant. They want us to take Joel to Prospector Point for a visit next weekend."

"I'm guessing you're not too keen on the idea."

"If he's really interested in meeting his grandson, shouldn't he come here?"

"Maybe. But if we go there, we can leave whenever we want," she pointed out.

"There's a plus," he acknowledged.

"But it's your decision," Erin said. "You're the only one who can say if this is something you want to do."

"But you have some thoughts," he guessed.

She shrugged. "Regardless of your relationship with him, he *is* Joel's grandfather. And until your mom agrees to marry Niall, he's the only grandfather that Joel has."

"My mom isn't going to marry Niall," he said.

Not that he objected to her having a relationship, he just couldn't imagine her making such a drastic lifestyle change after so many years on her own. Or maybe that was the reason she wanted to make a change.

But he pushed those thoughts aside for now to refocus on the conversation with Erin. "You think I should encourage a relationship, but I don't want our son to be disappointed when his grandfather loses interest."

"Is that what you think happened—why he left?" she asked gently. "Do you think he lost interest in being a dad?"

"No," he denied. Then, "I don't know."

"I'm beginning to realize that your relationship with your dad is probably as screwed up as mine with my mom."

"And that's probably why we're both determined to be better parents to our son," he acknowledged.

"Which is why I'm confident that when you fall in love and have a family with someone else in the future, you'll never let Joel feel as if he comes second."

"I'm not going to fall in love with someone else," he told her.

"You don't know that," she chided. "Just because it hasn't happened yet doesn't mean that it won't."

But Kyle did know—because he was already more than halfway in love with Erin.

And wasn't that realization an even bigger shock than his father's appearance at the restaurant today?

In the two weeks that had passed since Mother's Day, Kyle hadn't kissed her again. Obviously he'd taken the hint that she didn't want to complicate their relationship, and she was relieved he'd respected her decision.

The kiss they'd shared had been a mistake—not because she didn't want him but because she did. Because kissing him stirred up all kinds of feelings inside and made her want all manner of things she couldn't have. And since that kiss, she'd found herself wondering *what if* all over again.

What if she stopped ignoring the sparks that zinged between them whenever they were in the same room together?

What if she admitted that she wanted everything he was offering?

What if she confessed that she loved him?

What if she told him the truth about why she couldn't marry him and ruined everything?

As they fell back into a familiar routine that included Kyle spending every free minute with their son, he spent a lot of those minutes with Erin, too.

During those times, it was almost like they were a family, and it tempted her with the possibility of what might be.

To give herself a little bit of distance and perspective, Erin had been meeting more regularly with her clients, and Joel would hang out with his daddy while she was gone. Some days she and Kyle barely crossed paths, but at other times, he'd hang out for a while and they'd talk not just about Joel but his job and her job and all manner of other things. But he hadn't brought up the topic of marriage again.

She was relieved, of course. And maybe just the tiniest bit disappointed.

And now she was annoyed—albeit for a completely different reason.

"What did you do to my kitchen?" she demanded, when Kyle returned to her apartment after being summoned by a text message.

"What do you mean?"

"I can't open my cutlery drawer." She yanked it again in frustration, rattling the contents inside but making no progress in her efforts to access them. "Or any of my drawers or cupboards."

"Oh." He had the good sense to look chagrined. "I forgot to tell you—I had them childproofed."

"You had my drawers and cupboards childproofed?" she echoed.

"Mine, too," he said. "I wanted to make sure Joel will be safe when he's at my place, too."

"You do realize it's going to be a while before

he's walking—or even crawling—and trying to open drawers and cupboards."

"I know. But if even half the stories I've heard Liam tell about his kids are true, by the time we actually need these safety measures, Joel will be keeping us too busy to get them done."

"Liam has three kids," she reminded him. "Triplets. We have one four-month-old who wants his dinner, but I can't get a bowl or spoon to make his cereal."

"You just slide your finger in the gap and press to release the catch," he said, demonstrating for her.

"Thank you," she said, reaching into the drawer for one of the plastic baby spoons.

Anticipating, he opened the cupboard overhead and handed her a plastic bowl.

"Did it ever occur to you to ask me before you locked me out of my own kitchen?"

"It did, but I knew you were meeting with a new client today and I didn't want to interrupt."

"*Potential* new client," she reminded him. "And why did it have to be done today?"

"Because Ron Lawson was already here, fixing a leaky pipe downstairs for Mrs. Powell."

Which all sounded perfectly reasonable, and yet she couldn't shake her irritation.

"Did your meeting not go well?" he asked.

"The meeting was fine."

"Then why are you making such a big deal over a few latches?"

"I don't know." She sighed. "I do know."

"Do you want to share?" he asked cautiously.

"Ignore me," she said instead. "I'm just tired. I didn't get much sleep last night."

"Was Joel restless?"

"No, I was. Because I couldn't stop thinking about your ridiculous proposal."

"Did you want to change your answer to the question?" he asked, his tone hopeful.

"No." Her response was blunt and firm.

"Are you sure? It seems to me you wouldn't have lain awake thinking about it if you weren't considering the potential benefits of a legal union."

"There you go again, turning my head with romantic talk."

"I can do romance, if you want romance."

She shook her head. "What I want is six hours of uninterrupted sleep."

"I can do that, too," he said.

"How?"

"I'll stay here tonight and deal with Joel when he wakes up."

"I appreciate your willingness to pinch-hit," she told him. "But as soon as he wakes up, I wake up."

"You won't hear him—because you're going to be upstairs in my apartment."

She was intrigued by the offer, but still more than a little hesitant.

"You can trust me to take care of our son for one night," he assured her. "And if anything comes up that I can't handle, I'll know where to find you."

The prospect of uninterrupted sleep beckoned enticingly. "I have always wanted to try out your bed."

"All you had to do was ask," he said, with a teasing wink.

Erin rolled her eyes. "I didn't mean because it's yours. Only because it's so big."

"Stop—you're making me blush."

But really, she was the one whose cheeks were hot. *"The king-size bed,"* she clarified.

"Oh. Right."

Though she wasn't sure that she'd be able to sleep so far away from Joel, she decided it would be foolish to turn down this opportunity to at least give it a try.

"I'll have my phone right beside the bed," she told him.

"I won't call," he promised.

She smiled then. "Thank you."

He kissed her forehead. "Go get some sleep."

Of course, she checked on the baby one last time before she said good-night to Kyle and headed upstairs. It felt odd being in his apartment when he wasn't there.

Odder still to pull back the covers and climb into his bed.

She just wanted to sleep, but thanks to his pointed innuendo—and no doubt he'd have something to say about that word choice, too—she worried that she'd lie awake thinking about all the other fun things that could happen in his king-size bed if he was there with her.

She was out as soon as her head hit the pillows.

* * *

"I know your mom really likes waffles, but we're going to go with pancakes this morning," Kyle said to Joel, who was seated in his high chair so he could watch his dad putter around the kitchen. "Because she doesn't have a waffle iron and I'm afraid that if I go upstairs to get mine, I'll wake her up."

The baby gurgled.

Funny, Kyle wouldn't have thought gurgle was a real world, but the sound his son made was definitely a gurgle.

"I'll bet you'd love a pancake, too," Kyle said, as he measured and mixed ingredients. "But I think you need to stick with mushy stuff for a while yet."

Joel responded with a babble this time.

He was still a long way from making recognizable sounds, but Erin had assured Kyle that their son was making progress, that the gurgles and babbles and coos—and even the raspberries—were evidence that he was trying to communicate.

Of course, his most effective form of communication was crying, and Kyle had been jolted awake—twice—in the middle of the night by piercing screams so loud he'd worried that Erin might hear them even in his apartment upstairs.

Joel didn't stay awake for long either time, but Kyle had to be fully awake to change his diaper and warm his bottle. And each time after the baby was settled again, it had taken him a while longer to drift off. And while Kyle didn't feel too bad this morning, he was cognizant of the fact that he'd only dealt with the baby's demands for one night. Considering that Erin had been doing it every night since Joel was born, it was no wonder that she was exhausted.

He hoped that she'd slept well, with no one in the next room to disturb her slumber. But mostly he hoped that she'd awake refreshed and able to appreciate the benefits of having someone around to share the responsibility of nighttime feedings, which they'd more easily be able to do when they were married and living together.

She came in just after eight o'clock, wearing flannel pajamas and a huge smile.

"Nine hours," she said by way of greeting. "I slept for nine uninterrupted hours and it was wonderful."

"That's great," he said.

"Of course, when I woke up after nine hours, it was excruciating, because I've never gone that long without nursing—or at least pumping. So I used your shower, because warm water can help with letdown and—you really don't need all the details, do you?"

"Probably not," he said. "Although, it mostly sounds like you're speaking a foreign language, anyway."

She managed to laugh. "It's okay. I got nine hours of sleep. I didn't think it would happen, but it did and I'm *so* grateful to you."

"You're welcome?"

"I sound like a crazy person, don't I? I just have so much energy—it's as if my batteries are fully recharged. And you made breakfast for me, too," she realized.

"Pancakes," he said, taking the platter out of the oven and setting it on the table. "Because you don't have a waffle iron."

"Mmm...and sausage." She took a seat at the table and immediately began transferring food to her plate. "You know you played the wrong card when you suggested we get married."

"What card should I have played?"

She gestured to her plate with her fork. "This one."

"Are you saying that you would have given me a different answer if I promised to ensure that you'd never go hungry?"

"Probably not," she admitted, as she dug into her pancakes. "But I would have given it serious consideration."

"Food for thought," he said.

Chapter Sixteen

Since Tuesday was Kyle's day off from the restaurant, Erin tried to schedule client meetings and other appointments on that day, when he was available to take care of Joel. He never admitted to her that he'd been absolutely terrified the first few times he was left alone with the little guy, certain that he'd do something wrong or otherwise screw up and make her decide that he couldn't be trusted with their child.

But after a few weeks, he'd learned to read the baby's cues. He could even tell by Joel's cries if he was hungry or wet or tired. So Kyle was feeling pretty confident in his parenting skills when he waved goodbye to Erin on the last Tuesday morning in May. In fact, he was thinking that he might take Joel to the farmers market again so that he could look around at all the colors and scents—a first step, Kyle hoped, toward understanding and appreciating that quality ingredients made good food.

But Joel slept for longer than usual that morning, and when he did wake up, his cries sounded different.

"You were tired today," Kyle said, lifting the baby out of his crib and laying him down on the change table. "Did you not sleep well last night?

"Mommy didn't say anything about you having a restless night," he said, as he unsnapped the baby's sleeper, "but she had a big meeting this morning, so she was probably already focused on that."

He peeled back the diaper shirt and laid his hand on Joel's belly to hold him in place while he swapped out the wet diaper for a dry one.

"Hmm." Kyle frowned at the heat emanating from the baby's skin. "I don't think this is normal."

And the baby's lack of engagement wasn't normal, either. Usually his eyes were intent on Kyle's face when he was talking to him, but today Joel was completely uninterested, not even gurgling in response to his dad's chatter.

"Let's check your temperature and see if there's reason to panic."

101.2

Kyle panicked.

And then he tried to call Erin, but her phone went straight to voice mail, which increased his sense of alarm.

But what could she do even if she'd answered his call? She was in Battle Mountain today—too far away to return home quickly. Most likely she'd tell him to call the pediatrician, so he did that.

And then he called his mom.

"I was just about to leave for the restaurant," Jo said when she connected the call.

"I'm sorry," Kyle said. "But Erin's at a meeting and Joel's running a fever and—"

"What's his temperature?"

"101.2."

"Has the pediatrician okayed baby Tylenol?"

"I just talked to Dr. Tahir, and that's what he recommended, but I can't find any in the medicine cabinet."

"I'll be there in ten minutes."

"Thanks," he said, but she'd already hung up.

He exhaled a weary sigh of relief as he set down his phone.

He didn't feel like a failure because he'd had to reach out for help. He'd rather acknowledge his own shortcomings than risk anything happening to Joel. And truthfully, he'd considered bundling up the baby and driving to the hospital, so he figured he deserved some credit for opting for a more reasonable and rational response in calling his mom.

Thankfully, she was at the door in less than the ten minutes she'd promised, with a paper bag from the pharmacy in hand.

"Thanks for coming," he said.

"Of course." She was already halfway across the room to where Joel was secure inside his bouncy chair, paying no attention to the toys he usually loved. But his expression brightened a little when his saw his grandmother, and he even managed to produce a gummy smile.

"There's Grandma Jo's big boy," she said, unbuckling his harness and lifting him into her arms. "Your cheeks are definitely flushed," she noted, then touched her lips to his forehead. "And you feel a little warm. Did you pick up a bug when you were out and about this week?"

"I took him to the market last week," Kyle confided now. "Is this my fault?"

"It's no one's fault," his mom assured him. "Babies' immune systems aren't very well developed, so they get sick easily and often."

He read the instructions on the box of medication, then carefully measured out the appropriate dosage. He was relieved when Joel let him put the dropper in his mouth and squirt the medication onto his tongue. Then he picked up the thermometer again to check the baby's temperature.

Jo chuckled. "You might want to give the medication more than thirty seconds to work."

"How much more?"

"At least half an hour."

He looked at his watch, nodded.

"Counting down the minutes won't make them go any faster," she said. "And if you're anxious, Joel's going to feel anxious, too."

"How can I not be anxious? He's sick and—"

"He's going to be just fine," she interjected to assure him.

"How can you be sure?"

"Because I refuse to consider any other possibility."

"Is that the secret to successful parenting— positive thinking?"

"I don't know that it's a secret, but it's an essential tool," she told him. "Doctors can offer reassurance and pharmaceuticals, but in the middle of the night, sometimes hopes and prayers are all a parent's got. I can't tell you how many nights I sat up with you and your sister, hoping and praying that whatever ailed you would pass."

And she'd done it on her own. Maybe not in the beginning, but Marty was gone before Lucy's fifth birthday, leaving Jo alone to pick up the shattered pieces of her family and try to put them back together.

It wasn't until he was much older that Kyle learned the details of his parents' marriage. That in the early years, Jolene had worked at Haven Pizzeria to help make ends meet while her husband was getting his landscaping business of the ground. Right around the time of her divorce, the previous owners decided to sell the restaurant. Though she'd apparently been reluctant to take on the hefty mortgage that would be required for her to buy the business, she didn't see that she had any choice if she was going to provide for her family as the child support awarded by the court didn't amount to much of anything.

At the same time, she'd moved her family into the two-bedroom apartment over the pizzeria (renamed Jo's Pizza) while his dad's other family lived in luxury. It wasn't the pinching pennies that bothered Kyle so much as the fact that, at ten years of age, he was suddenly responsible for looking after his five-year-old sister whenever their mom was working—and it seemed as if she was always working!

When Kyle wasn't taking care of Lucy, he'd been helping out in the restaurant—bussing tables or washing dishes. And they were always eating pizza or pasta for dinner, because Jo didn't have time to make anything else, although she usually insisted that they have salad or some other kind of vegetable with it. Was it any wonder then that Kyle, with the assistance of YouTube videos, had expanded upon the basics his mom had taught him and learned how to cook actual meals?

And once he'd mastered some simple recipes and cooking methods, he'd begun to experiment—changing up ingredients and adding different spices. His mom had been his biggest fan, always happy to sample whatever he'd prepared and exclaim about its deliciousness, promising that she'd let him have free rein in her restaurant kitchen someday.

But when he'd expressed an interest in going to culinary school, Jo was baffled. Why did he want to go away when she could teach him everything he needed to know about making the world's best pizza (and according to all the local residents, Jo's Pizza was the best) in her own kitchen?

He'd returned to Haven with his diploma and the expectation that his mom would let him expand the offerings at Jo's beyond pizza, wings and simple pasta dishes. But the heart of the business had always been pizza, and she'd been reluctant to venture too far away from that basic menu. Despite the fact that she'd reneged on their agreement, she was furious when Kyle had chosen to take a job at another restaurant, where he'd hoped to have more freedom and creativity. Duke hadn't balked when he wanted to try new things, but Diggers' customers were less forgiving.

Liam Gilmore's decision to open an upscale dining facility in his newly renovated hotel had proved to be a smart one, and Kyle was thrilled to have complete control over the menu. Especially since it was the only part of his life that he had any control over these days.

"This parenting thing is scary," he confided now.

"It's terrifying," his mom agreed. "And also fun and exciting and frustrating and satisfying and all the other emotions you've ever known."

"How did you do it on your own?"

"It wasn't always easy," she acknowledged. "But you and your sister have always been my pride and joy."

"Did you ever wish Dad had helped out more?"

She laughed then. "Every day and twice on Sundays. But the truth is, we mostly managed okay. And if he wasn't there to help through the tough times, he wasn't there to share the good times, either, and that's his loss, because there were a lot more good times.

"Still, I'm glad to know that he's making an effort now, though I wish Lucy wasn't sneaking off to Prospector Point to see him."

"I know that she's been in contact with him," he hedged. "I wouldn't say that she's been sneaking."

"When you're not honest about what you're doing, it's sneaking," she insisted.

"If she wasn't honest with you, it was probably only because she didn't want to hurt you."

"I don't care that she's been seeing him," Jo said, then shook her head. "No, that's not true. I'm *happy* that she's been seeing him."

"You don't sound happy," Kyle said cautiously.

"I'm not happy that she thought she had to hide her visits," his mom explained. "I never wanted to keep you and your sister from your father."

"Then I should tell you that Dad wants to meet Joel, and we've been invited to Prospector Point this weekend. Of course, we'll have to see how the baby's feeling before we decide whether or not to go."

"He's going to be fine," Jo said again. "By Saturday, this crisis will be a distant memory for you and completely forgotten by him. Don't use it as an excuse not to go to Prospector Point."

"You want us to go?"

"I do," she confirmed. "I spent a lot of years being mad at Martin because he wasn't there for you and Lucy. But the truth is, he might have been there more if I hadn't made it so difficult for him. And I might not have spent a lot of years feeling guilty for depriving you of a relationship with your father."

"He didn't try very hard to be there for us," Kyle pointed out, admittedly still a little bitter about that fact.

"He could have tried harder," she agreed. "And I

could have been more accommodating. But there's no purpose in regrets now."

"Hmm."

"Why are you asking about that now? Dare I let myself hope that you're finally thinking about marriage?"

"I haven't had a lot of luck making relationships work," he confided.

"Work makes relationships work," his mother told him. "Luck doesn't have anything to do with it."

"I want me and Erin and Joel to be a family," he said. "But she's made it clear that she has no intention of marrying me just because we made a baby together."

Jo shook her head. "I sometimes wonder how such a smart man can be so oblivious."

"What is it you think I'm oblivious about?"

"The fact that you love her."

"Of course, I love her. We were friends for a long time before…"

"Before you fell into bed together?" she finished for him.

He nodded.

"So you're telling me that you love her as a friend?"

"She *is* a friend," he said again.

"I was wrong. You're not oblivious, you're an idiot."

Joel bounced back quickly from whatever it was that had ailed him. Of course, Erin took him to the doctor the next day "just to be on the safe side," but the little guy was already brighter and happier, more like his usual self by then.

"I'm sorry you had to deal with a feverish baby," she said. "But I'm glad you reached out to your mom."

"She seemed the obvious choice, when I couldn't reach you. Plus, she totally dotes on her grandson."

"And he lights right up when he hears her voice."

"If I'd known having a baby was all I needed to do to soften her attitude toward me, I might have knocked you up years ago," he teased.

She lifted her brows. "You think I would have let you get into my pants years ago?"

His lips curved as his gaze skimmed over her in a leisurely and sensual perusal that made her whole body tingle. "Yeah, I do."

And heaven help her, he was probably right.

Of course, Joel's quick recovery meant that Kyle had no excuse to cancel their plans to visit his dad and stepmom on Saturday morning—until Claudio called to tell them that they were heading to the hospital because Lucy was in labor.

"What do you think?" Kyle asked Erin, as he buckled Joel into his car seat. "Prospector Point or the maternity ward at the hospital?"

"You have no idea how long babies take to be born, do you?"

"No," he admitted.

"Prospector Point," she said. "We'll visit with your dad and stepmom as planned and stop by the hospital on our way home to see your sister and brother-in-law, then we'll go back again tomorrow to meet their son or daughter, because chances are, the baby won't be born before then."

"You really think it's going to take that long?" he asked skeptically.

"Every baby is different," she acknowledged. "But I was in labor for sixteen hours with Joel."

"Wow."

She nodded.

"Who kept you company for those sixteen hours?" he asked.

"My mom."

Knowing what he did about her relationship with her mother, he was understandably taken aback by this revelation. "Was that your choice?"

"Not my first choice," she admitted. "Anna was my partner for childbirth classes, but she and Nick had gone to Jonesboro for his grandmother's hundredth birthday that weekend. She offered to stay, because it was so close to my due date, but I couldn't let her miss such a milestone occasion. Plus, I knew that she and Nick needed a break from everything, and everyone I'd talked to assured me that first babies are always late."

"When was he due?" Kyle asked.

"February fourth."

He knew, because she'd given him a copy of the baby's birth certificate, that Joel was born on the thirtieth of January, but Kyle hadn't given any thought to whether he'd been early or late or on time.

"So because he decided to come five days early, you ended up in the delivery room with your mom?"

"It made sense to have someone with me who'd been through labor and childbirth before and—" Erin shrugged "—she offered. Actually, I think my dad might have nudged her into making the offer, but she was surprisingly supportive.

"Apparently she started to do a lot of reading on postpartum depression after Anna told her that she was pregnant, because she was worried that Anna might struggle to bond with her baby—like my mom did with me. She even apologized for not making more of an effort, which I really thought might be a turning point in our relationship.

"Until the next day, when she came back to the hospital and found me crying—not for any particular reason except that I was overwhelmed by hormones and emotions—and tried to reassure me that it was okay if I didn't love my baby, that feelings of maternal affection would eventually come if I spent enough time with him. Which was both hurtful and insulting, because I already loved Joel more than anything in the world."

"And it shows in everything you do," he assured her. "Every day I watch you with him, I realize our son is incredibly lucky to have you as a mom."

"I'm the lucky one," she said. "He's such a good baby."

"Are you saying that you'd love him less if he was a difficult baby?"

"Of course not," she said.

He'd only been teasing her, but the almost imperceptible pause before she responded made him realize it was something she'd not only considered but worried about. That she'd been afraid she might reject her baby, as she felt her mom had rejected her.

"My dad was great, though," she said. "He wasn't particularly happy when I told him I was pregnant and that the baby's dad wasn't in the picture—although I assured him that was my choice—but he was excited about being a grandpa again. And, of course, he fell head over heels the first time he held Joel."

"Because our kid is magic that way," Kyle said.

She smiled at his matter-of-fact tone. "I'm just glad my dad got to meet him. I only wish he'd had the chance to meet you, too."

"I would have come to Silver Hook at any time if you'd asked."

"I know," she admitted now. "And I should have asked. I should have done a lot of things differently."

He couldn't disagree. And it frustrated him to think about how different things might be now if she'd told him about her pregnancy when she first knew.

On the other hand, she'd had his baby, so he had a lot to be grateful for, too.

Joel worked his magic again when he was introduced to Grandpa Marty, Grandma Mandy, Uncle Duncan, Uncle Callum and Aunt Fiona, and at the end of a surprisingly enjoyable visit, Kyle and Erin promised to bring him back soon.

"That wasn't so bad, was it?" Erin asked, when they were in the car heading toward home.

"No," he acknowledged. "But that might have been because Duncan, Callum and Fiona were there."

"They wanted to meet your son—and probably see you, too," she added teasingly.

"I haven't made much of an effort to keep in touch with them," he acknowledged.

"Because spending time with them makes you feel disloyal to your mom?" she guessed.

"Maybe."

"She and your dad have been divorced…how long?"

"Twenty-five years."

"I think it's fair to assume she's moved on with her life," Erin said. "She certainly seems happy enough with Niall these days."

"Apparently," he agreed. "But that's something I'd rather not talk about."

Her phone buzzed inside her pocket, and she pulled it out to glance at the screen.

"Well, it's a girl," she told him.

"What?" he asked, clearly baffled by the sudden announcement.

"Lucy had the baby."

Her thumbs moved over the keypad as she composed a response to Claudio's message, adding lots of celebratory emojis and hugs and kisses.

"Three hours," she said, shaking her head. "It's

only been three hours since Claudio texted to say they were on their way to the hospital."

"You shouldn't really be surprised," Kyle said. "You know my sister. When she wants something to happen, she makes it happen."

"Still... I've never heard of anyone delivering a baby that quickly. Not that I wanted her to suffer through a longer labor," she hastened to clarify. "I just can't believe it was so fast."

Although, considering how long it had taken her friend to conceive, how many home pregnancy tests she'd bought and how many tears she'd shed when the results weren't what she'd hoped, perhaps it was fitting that at least one part of it had been easy for Lucy.

Of course, they stopped at the hospital on their way home. And though baby visitors weren't usually allowed on the maternity ward—with the exception of siblings—the nurses obligingly looked the other way when Kyle and Erin snuck Joel in to meet his brand-new cousin.

"Six pounds twelve ounces and eighteen inches," the proud new dad announced.

"And absolutely gorgeous," Erin said, cuddling the newborn.

"Lucky for her, she looks just like her mom," Claudio said.

"That is lucky," Kyle teased his brother-in-law.

"Does she have a name yet?" Erin asked.

"Seraphina Belle," Lucy said, smiling.

"Because she's our beautiful angel," Claudio explained.

They didn't stay long, because Kyle had to go into work for the dinner shift and, more important, the new mom needed to rest, but it was a nice visit, though Erin was feeling decidedly melancholy when they left the hospital.

After Joel was secured in the backseat but before she could open the passenger-side door of the vehicle, Kyle tipped her chin up, forcing her to meet his gaze. "Tell me what's wrong."

"Nothing's wrong."

"Then why do you look as if you're trying not to cry—and failing," he amended, as the first tears spilled over her lashes and slid down her cheeks.

"They're happy tears," she said, brushing them away. "Mostly."

"Because?" he prompted.

"Because Lucy and Claudio waited a long time to have a baby, and—" her voice cracked a little "—I'm so happy for them."

He waited, as if he knew that wasn't the whole reason for her tears.

"I'm happy for them," she said again. "But seeing them together, I'm a little envious, too. Because despite all the heartache they went through trying to have a baby, they went through it together. And when Lucy finally got pregnant, they celebrated together. And today, they brought their beautiful little girl into the world together."

"And you were on your own," he noted.

"Not entirely. But I did it all without you. I *chose* to do it without you," she acknowledged. "And listening to Claudio talk about cutting the cord when Seraphina was born—hearing the awe and wonder in his voice—I realized how much you missed out on because I decided not to tell you that we were having a baby."

"I do wish you'd told me you were pregnant," he said. "And I would have loved to have been there when our son was born, but that's all water under the bridge now."

"I wasn't sure you'd want to be there." She whispered the confession. "And maybe that's one of the reasons I never told you that I was pregnant. Because as long as you didn't know, I could tell myself that you would have come if you'd known, and that the only reason you didn't come was that you didn't know. Not because you didn't want our baby."

"If you'd asked me to come, I would have been there—even if Joel wasn't my baby," he said now. "Because friends are there for one another, no matter the circumstances."

"Are we still friends?"

"Always," he promised.

It was more than she deserved, but not even a fraction of what she wanted.

Chapter Seventeen

Friday afternoon, Erin was taking advantage of Joel's nap time to draft invoices for recent projects. It was her absolute least favorite part of the job, but it needed to be done. When a knock sounded on the door, she was grateful for the reprieve. Since she'd moved back to Haven, there had been no shortage of visitors stopping by to welcome her home—and get a peek at her (and Kyle Landry's!) baby.

She didn't really mind. Especially since no one ever came empty-handed. "New moms don't have time to be fussing over the stove," she'd been told every time she accepted yet another stew or casserole or pie. Because even those who knew her well were too polite to acknowledge that she'd never spent much time in the kitchen even before she'd had a baby.

Mrs. Powell, her downstairs neighbor, was one of the more regular visitors. But Helen never stayed long—especially if Joel was napping when she dropped by. "You should be resting when he does," she'd advised the new mom. "Not entertaining old ladies who have nothing better to do with their time."

Erin appreciated the sentiment, but she also sincerely enjoyed spending time with the widow who'd lived in Haven her whole life and had a story to tell about every single one of the town's residents. Mrs. Powell didn't gossip, though. She wouldn't ever break a confidence or say anything mean-spirited.

Erin sniffed her shoulder as she made her way to the door, checking to see if she smelled like baby spit. Because she hadn't had a chance to take the burp cloths out of the dryer before she'd nursed Joel earlier that morning and, of course, he'd spit up on her. She added "laundry" to the mental list she'd been compiling of all the things she needed to do while the baby was down for his nap as she opened the door.

"Mom." Erin honestly would not have been more surprised if she'd discovered Bozo the Clown standing outside her door. "What are you doing here?"

Bonnie's smile was as tentative as her tone. "Well, that's not quite the welcome I was hoping for, but I guess that's my fault for not telling you that I was coming."

"I'm happy to see you," Erin said, offering her mother an awkward hug. "I'm just surprised. Haven isn't a leisurely drive from Silver Hook."

"I know," Bonnie agreed. "I flew into Elko and drove from there."

"Is everything okay?" she asked cautiously.

"No. I mean yes. But not really. Nothing has been the same since your dad passed away."

Erin knew that was true. Not a day went by that she didn't think about and miss her dad. It wasn't even as if she'd been in the habit of talking to him every day—but it had been comforting to know that he was there if she needed him. And now he wasn't. She could only imagine how much harder it was for her mom to suddenly be without her husband of forty-two years, to live every day in the house that had been their home together and to sleep alone in the bed they'd shared.

"I thought I was doing okay," Bonnie continued. "I thought keeping busy at the resort would be good for me. But there are so many memories of him every way I turn. And, of course, most of our guests are return visitors, who all want to share their memories, and I just needed a break from it all.

"Diana Locke suggested that I book a solo vacation to visit art galleries in France or vineyards in Italy. Apparently that's something that a lot of older people—divorced or widowed—" her voice trembled on the word "—do, but I'm not sure I'm up for something like that. Or that I should go too far away or be gone for too long, expecting Ian and Marissa and Anna and Nick to be responsible for the resort. So I decided to start with something a little closer to home. And since Arkansas is closer to Nevada than it is to Oregon, here I am."

"Here you are," Erin agreed. And while "For how long?" and "Where are you planning to stay?" were the questions at the forefront of her mind, she refrained from blurting them out lest she give her mom the impression she wasn't welcome.

But some advance notice would have been nice. If she'd known Bonnie was going to show up at her door, Erin might have wiped the bread crumbs off the counter, folded the laundry in the basket on the sofa—or at least moved it out of sight—and changed into a clean shirt. Not that any of those things really mattered, but she was suddenly aware of each incomplete task as her mother's gaze swept around the room.

"How is my youngest grandson?" Bonnie asked.

Erin's smile came easily this time. "He's doing great. We just started him on cereal, which he absolutely loves. And he's rolling over—only front to back, so far, but I'm sure back to front won't be long."

"Anna showed me the video you sent to her."

"I sent it to you, too," Erin said.

Her mother waved a hand. "You know I'm not really good with technology."

"Clicking an attachment in an email isn't really a technological challenge."

"You always tell me not to click on attachments."

"If they're from someone you don't know," Erin clarified. "If it's a video file that comes from my email address with a message that says, 'Hey, Mom, check out this cute video of Joel,' you should feel pretty confident that it's a video from me and not a computer virus."

"Well, I did see the video," Bonnie reminded her. "And it was cute. Especially the look on his face when he suddenly found himself on his back, as if he wasn't quite sure how it had happened."

"Yeah, he surprised himself a few times in the beginning," she said. "Now he does it on purpose, and then he looks so proud of himself."

Bonnie smiled. "I hope I get to see him do it while I'm here."

"I'm sure you will," Erin agreed. "And you probably won't have to wait too long—he'll be up from his nap soon."

"He's sleeping now? Isn't it a little late in the day for a nap?"

"No, this is his usual afternoon naptime," she said, refusing to let her mother's obvious disapproval make her feel incompetent. Because the schedule worked for Joel—and for Erin and Kyle, too—and that was all that mattered.

"When you were a baby, we couldn't let you nap after three or you'd be awake until midnight."

"Was that me?" Erin asked. "Or Anna?"

"It might have been your sister," Bonnie acknowledged, her cheeks flushing at the reminder that she was pretty much checked out during the first two years of her oldest daughter's life.

"Well, we haven't had any trouble with Joel's schedule," she said, offering an olive branch.

"That's the second time you've said 'we,'" her mom remarked. "You mean you and Kyle?"

Erin nodded.

"So the two of you are together?"

"We're co-parenting."

"I don't know what that means," Bonnie admitted.

"It means that we're sharing the responsibilities and decisions that affect our son."

"But you're not together?"

"We're not together." Desperate to change the subject, she said, "Why don't we sit out on the balcony and enjoy the sunshine?"

"Okay," her mother agreed.

She opened the patio door, pleased when she heard her mother's breath catch as she took in the view of the mountains in the distance.

"Oh, that is a view," she said. "I guess I was so focused on following the directions on the car's navigation system, I didn't let myself appreciate how pretty it is out here."

Erin resisted the urge to shake her head over the fact that her mother could figure out the navigation system of a rental vehicle she'd never driven before but not how to open an email attachment on her own computer.

"Can I offer you something to drink?" she asked instead, silently willing her sleeping baby to wake up *now*.

"Do you have iced tea?"

"I do," Erin confirmed. "It's not sweetened, but I have sugar."

"That would be fine," Bonnie said. "But...will you hear Joel if we're outside?"

"I'll bring out the monitor," she said, trying not to bristle at the implication that she wouldn't have thought to do so.

"Okay."

She poured two glasses of tea over ice, added the sugar bowl and a long-handled spoon to the tray, and carried it outside.

"It really is a beautiful view," Bonnie noted again. "But I'm not sure it's safe to have a balcony with a baby."

"I lived here before I had a baby," she reminded her mom. "And it's not as if I leave him out here un-attended."

"Still, an apartment isn't really an ideal place to raise a child, is it?"

"He's got a roof over his head and food in his belly—I think he's happy enough."

"For now. But your apartment will start to feel small awfully fast as he grows up. No doubt he'd be happier with a backyard to run around in."

"And I'd be happier driving a Mercedes, but my Kia gets me where I need to go," Erin told her.

"Forgive me for showing an interest in my daughter's—and grandson's—life," Bonnie replied stiffly.

Erin sighed. "I don't have a problem with the interest, Mom, just the criticism."

"I always seem to say the wrong thing to you," her mother said, an acknowledgment more than an apology.

"We've never communicated very well," Erin noted.

"And that's my fault."

"I don't know that it's anyone's fault," she said. "It just is."

"It is my fault," Bonnie insisted, the spoon clinking against the side of the glass as she stirred sugar into her tea. "And that's another one of the reasons I'm here…to apologize for what I said to you after the funeral."

"It was a difficult week for everyone," Erin said, wondering why her mother's sudden desire to apologize had precipitated a sixteen-hundred-mile trip rather than a simple telephone call.

"You're being kinder than I deserve," her mom said.

Erin shrugged. "Being a mom is exhausting—I don't have the energy to hold a grudge."

But she hadn't been able to forget the words, or the feeling of a knife twisting in her gut. On the other hand, those harsh words had set her free, allowing Erin to leave Silver Hook without guilt or remorse, because she knew her mom neither needed nor wanted her there.

"We'd been making progress, though," Bonnie noted. "Even your dad remarked about it a few months earlier."

"He did?"

Her mom nodded. "He was so happy to see us getting along. Working side-by-side at the resort—even

in the kitchen on occasion. It was all so normal...
when nothing else was."

"There were a few bright spots in those dark
days," Erin agreed.

"I feel fortunate that Brian and I had so many
happy years together. There were some rough
patches, of course, including the first couple of years
after you were born."

Something else that her mom blamed her for, no
doubt, Erin suspected, though she didn't dare say
so aloud and risk undermining the shaky détente
they'd reached.

"Your dad didn't understand why I had no interest
in our new baby. Neither did I, to be honest. After all,
I'd already had two other babies, so we both knew I
was capable of doing everything a mom needs to do."

She sipped her tea before continuing. "Not only
was I capable, I was happy. I loved being a mom.
And when I was pregnant with you, I had no doubt
that I'd love being your mom, too. Then...well, you
know what happened after delivery."

Postpartum hemorrhage.

Erin had heard the story countless times over
the years—most often from her grandmother, who
wanted everyone to know that she'd been the one to
save the day after Bonnie nearly died giving birth to
Erin. Stella Napper had recounted her heroics with
pride, never considering—or maybe not caring—
that the story might make her granddaughter feel
guilty about something over which she'd had absolutely no control.

"Your grandmother was a big help," Bonnie acknowledged now. "Especially with your brothers. But it was your dad who stepped up in a big way. He was the one who got up in the night to feed you or change you. Whatever you needed, he was there, because I wasn't… I couldn't.

"I was so relieved to know that you were being taken care of. And, at the same time, I resented his complete focus on you." She swallowed another mouthful of tea. "I'm not proud to admit it, but there it is—I was jealous and resentful of my own daughter, because her father loved her and I… I struggled to feel the way I knew I should."

Her mom had never spoken to her so candidly before, and Erin was beginning to think she should have been grateful for that. Because this confession did nothing to make Erin feel better.

"I did love you. I *do* love you," Bonnie said now. "But it always seemed as if you were more your father's daughter than mine. He was the one you ran to when you skinned your knee or needed help with a school project. He was the one you always wanted to share your good news with first, and he was always so proud of you."

"Until I got pregnant," she noted.

It was the only time they'd really butted heads, and she hated knowing that she'd added to his stress when he was already dealing with so much. He'd urged her to tell the baby's father—to give him a chance to step up and do the right thing.

But Erin didn't believe that getting married for

the sake of a baby was the right thing. And in any event, she had more pressing matters to deal with—such as helping her dad get better so that he could walk her down the aisle when she did get married.

He'd rallied a little then, proving that he wanted that as much as she did. And when he'd finally accepted that his days were numbered, he'd told her that one of the things he most regretted was that he wouldn't have that chance. But he also told her that he was sorry for pushing the issue, because the forty-two years that he'd spent with the woman he loved were the happiest of his life, and he'd been wrong to suggest that she settle for anything less.

"He would have been happier if you'd been married before you had a child," Bonnie acknowledged. "But he was absolutely thrilled when Joel was born. And moved to actual tears when he heard that you'd given his name to his grandson.

"He was grateful, too, that you came home to support the family through his illness, but he was adamant that, no matter what happened with him, you wouldn't stay in Silver Hook.

"So what I said to you, after the funeral, about him not wanting you there was true. But it wasn't the whole truth. I should have told you the reason—and the reason is that he knew you wanted to do more with your life than work at the resort, and he wanted more for you. Because you'd worked too hard to become a web designer to give up your career," Bonnie explained. "He was never anything but proud of you. And… I'm proud of you, too."

Erin had to swallow around the lump in her throat before she could speak. "Why are you telling me this now?"

"Because it's long overdue. Because I never should have let you leave without clarifying what I said to you that day. And because my therapist warned me that I wouldn't be able to let go of my guilt and grieve properly until I was honest with you."

And the surprises just kept coming.

"You've been seeing a therapist?"

Bonnie nodded. "For a few months now. Marissa suggested it." Then she shook her head. "No, Marissa insisted on it. And I'm glad she did."

If your mom needs anything, we'll be there for her, Marissa had assured Erin before she left Silver Hook. Erin was grateful that her brother's wife had kept her word—and that Marissa had apparently known what her mother-in-law needed even before Bonnie did.

"I leave her office with my emotions raw every time," Bonnie confided. "But I'm finally dealing with things I should have dealt with a long time ago."

"I'm glad it's helping," Erin said sincerely. And then she finally ventured to ask the question that had been on her mind since she opened the door to her mother. "So...how long are you going to be in town?"

"Probably just a few days."

"Do you want to stay here?" If she said yes, Erin would have to sleep on the sofa, but considering the effort that her mom had undertaken to come all this way, she had to offer.

"Oh, no," Bonnie said. "I booked a room at The Stagecoach Inn."

Which suggested that her mom's trip hadn't been completely impulsive after all.

"You'll love the inn," Erin assured her. "Do you know what room you booked?"

"Apparently a room called 'Bonnie.' The woman I spoke to on the phone seemed quite amused by the coincidence."

"Instead of numbers, the rooms are identified by names of famous Western personalities," Erin explained to her. "From Annie Oakley to Wild Bill, with interesting details about their lives engraved on plaques in each room. Bonnie is on the first floor, beside Clyde, with an adjoining door for guests traveling together."

"Well, it's just me," Bonnie said, forcing a smile. "Which means that I get the queen-size sleigh bed all to myself." Her smile trembled a little. "Of course, I've got a bed all to myself at home now, but it's not a sleigh bed."

"If you've got time, you should try to get into Serenity Spa," Erin said, more unnerved than she wanted to be by that trembly smile. "The hot stone massage is amazing."

"Maybe we could both go, if you don't have any plans for tomorrow."

"Actually, I do have plans," Erin said apologetically. "Tomorrow is Lucy's surprise baby shower."

"That sounds like even more fun," her mom decided. "Can I go with you?"

"Um…sure."

"Then maybe—if you have time—you could take me shopping for a baby gift?"

Erin smiled. "Of course, we've got time."

And for the first time in as long as she could remember, she was glad to be able to spend it with her mom.

Chapter Eighteen

"So...your mom's in town," Kyle said by way of greeting, when he showed up at Erin's after the restaurant closed that night.

"Word travels fast."

"Out-of-towners are always a hot topic in Haven."

As Erin was well aware. She'd been an out-of-towner when she arrived for Lucy's wedding seven years earlier, a designation that had stuck for more than six months, and then she was "the new girl" for another two years after that.

"I'm just surprised that you never mentioned she was coming," Kyle continued.

"Trust me, I would have mentioned it if I'd known. But she actually got on a plane and then rented a car in Elko to drive the rest of the way here without even calling to tell me that she was coming."

"I obviously don't know your mom very well, but that seems...out of character."

"It's definitely out of character," Erin agreed. "Or maybe this is her new character. Losing my dad has forced her to stand on her own two feet, and I think she's been a little surprised to realize that she can."

"It sounds like you had a good visit then."

"It was good. I might even say cathartic."

"How long is she going to be in town?" he wondered.

"She was a little vague about her timeline. I think she's trying to decide if she wants to go back to Silver Hook or venture further west to visit Owen and Roger in Portland."

"Will you give your brother a heads-up if she decides to go to Oregon?"

"Nah." She shook her head, but a smile played at the corners of her mouth. "But I'll let Roger know."

The surprise shower was Jo's idea, but getting Lucy to The Home Station so that the new mom could be surprised was Erin's responsibility. She decided to stick close to the truth and tell her friend that they were meeting Quinn for lunch, so Lucy was taken aback to discover that The Home Station had been closed for a private event—with her baby as a guest of honor.

Erin was equally so when she saw that the room was decorated with streamers and balloons in both pink and blue. There were also two banners hanging side by side, one proclaiming "It's a Girl" and the other "It's a Boy"—because apparently it was a shower to celebrate not only Seraphina but Joel, too.

"Are you surprised?" Jo asked, as guests mixed and mingled around them.

"More than," Erin assured her.

"I wasn't sure I'd be able to pull it off," the proud grandmother confided. "It was Kyle's idea to tell you that the shower was for Lucy, because he knew you'd be so focused on keeping it a secret from her, you wouldn't suspect it was for you, too."

"He was right," she confirmed. "And it was a really lovely surprise. Thank you."

"It was my pleasure," Jo said. "Although, as happy as I am to show off both my new grandbabies, I have to confess that I feel a little bit guilty, too."

"Why?" Erin asked, smiling as she watched Kyle carry their baby around the room.

"Because I was so caught up in the excitement of planning this celebration for both of my grandbabies, I didn't even think to reach out to your mom."

"You shouldn't feel bad," Erin told her. "I've lived in Haven for seven years now and this is only the second time she's come to visit." And the first time had undoubtedly been at the insistence of Erin's dad, who'd wanted to see where their eldest daughter was living, because he'd been certain that the whole state of Nevada was populated with only gamblers and prostitutes.

"Well, she's here now," Jo pointed out. "And obviously happy to be spending time with her daughter and grandson."

"She does seem to be enjoying herself," Erin agreed cautiously. Since Bonnie's arrival in Haven the previous afternoon, Erin had seen a side of her mom she'd never seen before, but after thirty-plus years, she wasn't ready to drop her guard completely.

"You know, there's no distance that can't be spanned by a bridge, provided the foundation is solid enough," Jo said, repeating the words Erin had once said to her.

"Then I guess it's time to practice what I preach," she acknowledged. "But first, let's eat."

After the luncheon, as Erin chatted with friends and family and neighbors who'd come together to celebrate with the new parents and meet the babies, she couldn't help but feel grateful that she'd been accepted as part of the close-knit community, and she was sincerely happy to know that Joel would grow up here, surrounded by people who cared about him.

"Look at that," Erin said to Kyle, when he made his way through the crowd to join her. "You finally got your mom to come to The Home Station."

"Claudio's mom picked the location," he pointed out. "The only reason mine didn't object was that she didn't want to have to shut down the pizzeria over lunch on a Saturday."

Erin chuckled. "Well, she's here—and she ate the delicious meal that was served."

"Even the spinach and strawberry salad?" he asked.

"Even that," she confirmed.

He turned around then and tipped his head back, looking at the blue sky out the window.

"What are you doing?" she asked.

"Checking to see if there are pigs flying."

"I was tempted to do the same thing when my mom showed up at my door," she confided.

"But you're glad she came."

"I'm glad that we had a chance to talk," she allowed. "We've communicated more directly and honestly in the past eighteen hours than at any time in the previous eighteen years."

"That's good, isn't it?"

"It is," she agreed.

It had also been emotional and exhausting, but she really did feel as if they'd taken a big step toward establishing a more traditional mother-daughter relationship. And while Erin knew that she'd never share the same closeness with Bonnie that Anna shared with their mom, that was okay, too.

"Now, tell me what the two of you were talking about earlier," she said, undeniably curious about the nature of the tête-à-tête she'd witnessed.

"She cornered me," Kyle admitted. "Literally. I had nowhere to go."

"That doesn't answer my question," Erin pointed out.

"We talked about a lot of things," he hedged. "Haven, the hotel, the restaurant."

None of which explained why her internal radar had gone off when she'd spotted them together.

"Anything else?" she pressed.

"Actually, she did…um…want to know when… we're getting married."

Erin's gaze narrowed. "What did you tell her?"

He offered an apologetic smile and a shrug. "I told her that we haven't yet set a date."

Which, of course, meant that Erin would have to be the one to set the record straight.

She found her mom in conversation with Jo— making plans to have lunch together the next day.

Would wonders never cease?

After they'd confirmed the details, Erin took Bonnie's arm and steered her away for a private word.

"This is a lovely party, isn't it?" Bonnie asked, lifting her drink to her lips. "I'm so happy to see that you've made so many friends. I miss you at home, of course, but I feel better knowing that you've made a new home for yourself here."

Erin eyed the pale liquid in her mother's glass. "What are you drinking?"

"Sangria. And it's delicious." Bonnie offered her daughter a sip.

She shook her head. "How many glasses have you had?"

"Two? Three?"

A surprise to Erin, who'd never known her mother to consume more than a single glass of wine and only on special occasions. It also gave her hope that maybe Bonnie wouldn't remember that she'd brought up the topic of marriage with the father of her youngest grandson.

So she decided to set the subject aside for the moment, asking instead, "Did you enjoy your lunch?"

"It was delicious," Bonnie said. "In fact, while I was eating, it occurred to me that you could eat like that all the time if you married the chef."

So much for setting the subject aside.

"I'm not going to marry a man just because he knows his way around the kitchen," she told her mother.

"The fact that you made a baby together suggests that he also knows his way around the bedroom."

"Mom!" Erin said.

And then she laughed, because she was discovering that she liked this relaxed and open version of her mother.

Bonnie's gaze darted around the room. "I probably shouldn't have said that out loud, should I?"

"There isn't anyone here who doesn't know that Kyle is Joel's father," Erin assured her.

"But sex isn't a usual topic of conversation at social events."

"Maybe it should be."

Her mom frowned at the pale liquid in her glass. "I don't think I should have any more of this."

"Why not? You're not driving anywhere."

"Because I might get lost finding my way back to my room."

"I won't let that happen—I promise."

Bonnie touched a hand to Erin's cheek. "You're a much better daughter than I ever was a mother."

"I'm sure that's not true," she felt compelled to protest.

"It is," her mom insisted. "I should have done more. I should have tried harder."

Erin gave her a quick, impulsive hug. "We're both trying now, and that's what matters."

"You're right," Bonnie decided. "Now, let's go find that cute baby of yours so Grandma can give him lots more hugs and kisses."

The following Saturday morning, Kyle was contemplating his breakfast options when Erin sent a text message:

Can you come downstairs ASAP?

He closed the door of his refrigerator, shoved his feet into his shoes and took the stairs two at a time.

"That was fast," Erin said, when he burst into her apartment.

"You said ASAP."

"Oh." She offered up a sheepish smile. "I didn't mean to give the impression that it was anything urgent."

"Joel's okay?"

"He's fine." She gestured to the high chair, so that he could see for himself.

Kyle blew out an unsteady breath.

It was then he noticed that the table had been set, complete with place mat and linen napkin in a brass ring and a trio of sunny yellow gerbera daisies floating in a clear glass bowl.

"What is this?" he asked curiously.

"An early Father's Day celebration," she explained. "Since you have to work brunch tomorrow, we wanted to celebrate with you today."

"We?" He sat down near his son. "Was this your idea?" he asked Joel.

The baby responded by banging his rattle against the tray of his highchair.

"Ah, I see now. You're the musical entertainment."

"What he lacks in repertoire, he makes up for with enthusiasm," Erin said.

"You won't hear any complaints from me," Kyle promised.

"The original plan was to treat you to breakfast in bed," Erin confided. "But the logistics of getting the baby and the food upstairs were too daunting."

"This is great," he assured her. "I mean, now that my heart isn't threatening to jump out of my chest, it's great." And he was both touched and pleased that she'd made such an effort.

"I'm sorry about the message," she said again. "I just didn't want your eggs to get cold."

As she spoke, she scooped the eggs out of the frying pan onto a plate already arranged with several strips of crispy bacon and a couple of ripe tomato slices.

"This looks really good," he said, as she set the plate in front of him.

And it tasted good, too. The eggs were light and

fluffy and the bacon perhaps a little overcooked but still delicious. He even ate the tomato slices.

When his plate was clean, she brought out a bowl of fruit that included wedges of melon, bright red strawberries, dark purple grapes, chunks of juicy pineapple and slices of kiwi.

"A wise chef once told me to play to my strengths—and apparently I'm really good at cutting up fruit."

She was referring, of course, to the time that she'd been helping out in the kitchen at The Home Station and totally destroyed a whole pound of shrimp in her attempt to devein them. Though he hadn't been amused at the time, he chuckled softly now. "You've come a long way since then."

"I'm not sure that's true," she said ruefully. "But I appreciate the sentiment."

"And I appreciate that I didn't have to cook my own breakfast."

"We've got something else for you, too," Erin said, placing a wrapped package in front of him.

A book, he guessed, considering the size and shape.

He tore the paper off, surprised to see a picture of a newborn baby on the cover. The infant was swaddled in a blue blanket with a knitted blue cap on his head. Joel Brian Landry was printed across the bottom.

"I had no idea what to get for you, so when you mentioned wanting to see Joel's first baby pictures, I got the idea to put them together in a book."

He scrolled through the pages, marveling over every one. "This is fabulous."

"While you're looking at that, I'm going to change Joel and put him down for his nap," she said, scooping the heavy-lidded baby out of his chair. "Say 'Happy First Father's Day, Daddy.'"

Joel's only response was to rub his cheek against his mom's shoulder, a telltale sign that he was ready for sleep.

"Well, by next year he should at least be able to manage the 'Daddy' part," she said.

Kyle couldn't wait. And at the same time, he wasn't in any hurry for his baby to grow up. Sure, there would be new and exciting things to discover with his son at every age, but right now, every day was new and exciting for Joel, and that made every day new and exciting for Kyle, too.

When Erin returned to the kitchen, it was spotless. The leftover food put away, dishes tucked into the dishwasher, frying pans washed and even the counters wiped.

"You were supposed to be looking at baby photos, not tidying up the kitchen," she protested.

"And yet I managed to do both." He took her hands then and drew her toward him. "Thank you. Not just for breakfast, but for making me a dad."

"As I recall, that was a joint effort."

"I remember." He smiled as he tipped his head toward her. "Every intimate detail."

"Don't." The warning—or was it a plea?—was little more than a breathless whisper.

"Don't what?" he asked, sounding amused.

"Don't kiss me."

Even as the words tumbled from her lips, she swayed closer to him, tilting her chin so that her mouth was mere inches from his, and she knew that she wouldn't be able to fault him if he breached those inches.

But he didn't do so.

Not yet.

Instead he asked, "Why don't you want me to kiss you?"

"Because I can't think when you kiss me," she admitted.

"You have to know that telling me something like that only makes me want to kiss you again and again, until you can't remember any of the reasons that you think we're a bad idea."

"It's not that I think we're a bad idea. It's just that our relationship is already complicated enough without adding more layers."

"Maybe we should try and simplify things a bit by giving in to the feelings that we've been ignoring for the past few months?"

She rolled her eyes. "Of course, you'd argue in favor of that, because it would mean we get to have sex."

"You don't want to have sex?" The teasing light in his eyes combined with the half smile on his face assured her that he knew the answer to that question.

"I don't want to mess things up," she said, because it was true. "We've been doing a pretty good job, I think, co-parenting our son, and we need to focus on that. The best thing for him is for his mom and dad to get along."

"As I recall, we got along *very well* when we were naked and horizontal. Although, now that I'm thinking about it, I'll bet vertical would work, too."

Dammit, now she was thinking about it, too.

And when his lips finally touched hers, she gave up any pretense of resistance and gave in to the heat that pulsed in her veins.

Chapter Nineteen

Kyle drew Erin closer, and the already tight peaks of her nipples brushed against the hard wall of his chest, sending tingles of awareness dancing through her veins, making her ache and yearn. His hands skimmed down her back, then up again, a feather-light touch that somehow managed to both soothe and seduce.

As he deepened the kiss, she knew there would be no going back this time. She knew it and she was glad of it. Because she wanted him even more than the first time, because now she knew what to expect, the way he could make her feel. The way only he'd ever made her feel.

When they were both naked and he eased her down onto the bed, the friction of bare skin against bare skin was almost more than she could take. She was like a volcano ready to erupt—not just because it had been so long, but because this was *Kyle*.

And because this was Kyle, it was more than lust that made her heart pound and her knees weak. There had always been affection between them, but now there was love. She'd been fighting her feelings for a long time, but she had no doubts anymore.

He kissed her again. Deeply. Hungrily. Then his mouth moved away from hers to trail kisses along her jaw, down her throat, raising goose bumps on her flesh. At the same time, his hands were on another journey, tracing her curves and contours.

He cupped her breasts, so much fuller and more sensitive now as a result of the child she'd borne. His thumbs brushed over the aching peaks, making her gasp. When he replaced his hands with his mouth and suckled her nipples, she nearly came apart right then and there.

Instead, she arched her back and lifted her hips off the mattress, rubbing her pelvis against the hard length of his erection. He didn't take the hint but continued his leisurely exploration, kissing his way down her body. He nudged her thighs further apart, then lowered his head and put his mouth on her. He used his lips and his tongue, sucking and stroking and driving her wild.

She cried out then, she couldn't help it, and she definitely couldn't hold back the climax. She could only fist her hands in the sheets and hold on as endless waves of sensation washed over her.

Kyle had never seen anything more beautiful than Erin in the throes of passion. Her lips were swollen from his kisses, her cheeks flushed with excitement and her beautiful blue eyes unfocused.

But he wasn't done yet. Not even close. He continued to touch her and kiss her, guiding her toward the pinnacle of pleasure again. Wanting to give her more. Wanting to give her everything.

This time when they made love, he wanted her to know that they were making love. This wasn't just sex and it wasn't just one-time. This was the start of something new, the beginning, he hoped, of the rest of their lives together. Because being with Erin didn't just feel good, it felt right.

He was rock-hard and aching for her, but he knew that this was her first time since giving birth almost five months earlier, and he wanted to be sure she was ready. He had no doubt that she was eager. Her throaty moans and impatient hands were evident of that fact.

He sheathed himself in a condom and fought against the urge to bury himself deep. Instead, he eased into her, a fraction of an inch at a time, giving her body a chance to accommodate and accept the intrusion. When he was finally, completely, inside her, she lifted her hips off the mattress to pull him deeper, and the last remnants of control slipped out of his grasp. As he began to move, she met him stroke for stroke, and they joined together in synchronized rhythm, pushing ever closer to the edge of oblivion.

He held on as long as he could, waiting for her

to find her release again. Just when he was certain he could hold on no longer, she cried out, her inner muscles tightening around him, signaling her climax as he surrendered to his own.

Kyle didn't intend to drift off and only realized that he'd done so when the sound of rain penetrated his slumber. No, it wasn't rain. It was the shower.

Erin was in the shower.

He was instantly, fully awake, because if Erin was in the shower, that meant she was naked. And wet. And he suddenly remembered that they hadn't yet tried the vertical that he'd teased her about.

Though the sound of the water beckoned, he wanted to check on Joel first, to make sure the little guy was still sleeping. He was.

So Kyle tiptoed out of the nursery again and turned the knob on the bathroom door, grateful that it wasn't locked. He slid back the curtain and stepped into the narrow enclosure.

Erin gasped. "Kyle—what are you doing?"

"Conserving water."

"Since when did you become so environmentally conscious?" she challenged, but the way her eyes lit up as they skimmed over his body assured him that she didn't object to his presence.

"Since it gave me an excuse to join you in the shower," he told her. "Your very small shower."

"Well, I'm almost finished," she said. "So you can have it all to yourself."

"Are you?" He squirted body wash onto the puffy

sponge she'd hung on the tub spout and began to rub it over her back, creating a foamy lather.

"I *was* almost finished," she clarified.

"And I'm just getting started," he promised.

She sighed with pleasure as he washed her, slowly and very thoroughly.

"Isn't there a saying—'You wash my back, I'll wash yours'?" he asked, as he soaped up her breasts.

"I believe it's 'You scratch my back, I'll scratch yours,'" she said.

"You already did the scratching," he teased.

"I didn't hear you complaining at the time."

"I'm not complaining now," he assured her.

And he definitely wasn't complaining when she moved behind him to trail her lips over the red marks she'd put on his back.

Or when she examined his front, too, for good measure.

Erin had long been a fan of green initiatives, but after today, she was convinced that water conservation was of critical importance and that sharing her shower with Kyle was perhaps something that should be repeated in the future. Again and again.

She was still smiling when she walked into the kitchen to see what she had in the fridge for lunch— a task interrupted by frantic knocking on her door.

"I need your help." Lucy had her baby tucked in a sling around her body, a box of painting supplies in her hands and a tone of desperation in her voice. "Please."

"What can I do?" Erin asked.

"Help," her friend said again, dropping her supplies on the kitchen island. "Apparently holding open the palm of a three-week-old baby is a two-person job, because I've ruined two T-shirts already and Father's Day is tomorrow.

"Oh." She spotted the book that Kyle had left there earlier. "Is this for my brother?" She opened the cover without waiting for a response from her friend, smiling as she turned the pages. "He's going to love it."

"I do love it," Kyle confirmed, joining them in the kitchen. His hair was still damp from the shower and a satisfied expression—no doubt courtesy of their water play—was on his face.

Lucy's gaze shifted from friend to her brother, her eyes growing wide as the pieces clicked together in her mind.

"Ohmygod. You guys had sex."

"Considering that we have a child together, you have to know it's not the first time," Kyle remarked dryly.

"But that was more than a year ago. And you both said it was a one-time thing."

"And now the situation has changed," he said.

"Why?" Lucy demanded, looking to her friend now. "Why would you do this?"

Erin wasn't quite sure how to answer that question—or why the discovery that she and Kyle had been intimate seemed to cause his sister distress. On the other hand, Lucy had a three-week-old baby, and

Erin understood that her friend's emotions didn't need to make sense—what mattered was that she was obviously upset.

"Our personal relationship isn't any of your business," Kyle told her now.

"Not any of my business?" she echoed in disbelief. "You're my brother and Erin's my best friend. And you had sex."

"I don't understand," he said. "I thought you wanted me and Erin together."

"Wait a minute." Erin held up a hand. "It's a pretty big leap from a midday rendezvous to together."

"Is it?" Kyle asked.

Lucy shook her head. "See? You guys are going to screw this up, and then my nephew is going to be the one to suffer."

"We're not going to screw anything up," Erin promised, her fingers mentally crossed.

"I can't process all of this right now," Lucy said. As Seraphina began to cry, the baby's mom did, too, tears spilling onto her cheeks and dripping down her face. "It's Father's Day tomorrow and…"

Erin took her friend by the shoulders and gently guided her down the hall to the nursery. "Sit," she said, nudging her into the glider rocker and setting a box of tissues within reach. "I'll get rid of your brother and then we can talk."

Lucy nodded as she extricated her baby from the sling.

"Is she okay?" Kyle asked, obviously baffled and worried by his sister's behavior.

"Aside from dealing with an overload of hormones, she's fine," Erin assured him.

"Are you sure that's all it is?"

"Trust me," she said. "I've been there, done that. And if you'd been there in the first few weeks after Joel was born, you would have seen a lot more tears than that."

Of course, she hadn't given him the option of being there, and maybe she needed to remind them both of that fact to gauge his response and know if he'd well and truly forgiven her for the choices she'd made.

"Next time, I'll be there for you," he promised. "Every step of the way."

Next time.

Those two words dimmed a little bit of the shine from their morning, but she managed a smile as she put their son into the baby carrier Kyle was wearing, gave him a quick kiss and shoved him out the door.

She returned to the nursery with a tall glass of water and a cup of hot peppermint tea. "Your choice," she said, setting them both on the window ledge within easy reach. "But you need to stay hydrated."

Lucy nodded. "Thank you."

Erin sat on the floor, her back against the wall, and hugged her knees to her chest. "Do you want me to apologize for sleeping with your brother?"

Lucy took a moment to switch her nursing baby to the other breast before responding. "Are you sorry?"

"No," Erin said honestly. And though she knew

they were having a serious conversation, she couldn't hold back the smile that curved her lips. "It's hard to be sorry when my body is still tingling."

"Stop. Please."

"As if you didn't tell me, in a little too much detail, how amazing Claudio was after the first night you spent together."

"The big difference there is that Claudio isn't *your* brother," Lucy pointed out.

"True."

"I know you're both consenting adults and, technically, your personal relationship isn't any of my business," her friend acknowledged now. "But I love you both and I'm worried that if you get in too deep and things don't work out, someone's going to get hurt."

"You don't have to worry about me," Erin said. "I'm a big girl."

"And Kyle's a big boy, but even big boys get their hearts broken."

"I'm not going to break his heart."

"You don't think you could," Lucy realized. "But you don't know how lost he was when you were gone."

"Lost?" Erin echoed dubiously.

"I'm not sure how to explain it. I didn't realize myself how deeply your absence had affected him until you came back again."

"If he was different when I came back, it was no doubt because I brought our son with me."

"No. Well, yes," Lucy agreed "Obviously he dotes on Joel and loves being a dad. But aside from that, he's different when he's with you. You make him happy."

"When I'm not making him mad, you mean?"

Her friend smiled. "Yeah, but that's part of it, too. He's always been so completely in control, never letting anyone see what he's thinking or feeling. No doubt that's part of what makes him so good in the kitchen—he can juggle multiple tasks while still maintaining focus on the most minute details by blocking everything else out.

"Except you," Lucy noted. "He's never been able to block you out. Maybe he's never wanted to. Whether he's said the words or not, he loves you, Erin. And I know you love him, too."

"I do love him."

"But something's holding you back from telling him how you feel."

"I'm afraid he wants more than I can give him," she confided to her friend.

"He wants a life with you and Joel. A family."

It was what Erin wanted, too, except that she would have been perfectly happy as a family of three, while Kyle's remarks suggested otherwise.

And expanding their family wasn't an option.

Chapter Twenty

By the time Kyle and Joel returned from their banishment, aka "walk," Erin and Lucy were washing the paint off Seraphina's hands—and various other parts of her body.

"Everything okay?" he asked cautiously.

"The meltdown is over—for now, anyway," Lucy said.

Satisfied by her response, Kyle ventured into the kitchen to look at their handiwork. The T-shirt on the counter said Best Dad across the top and Hands Down near the bottom, with two tiny red handprints between the words.

"Cute," he said. "But you could have centered the handprints—or added more to fill up the space."

"I did it like that on purpose," his sister told him.

"So that there's room to add another set of hand-prints when we have another baby, and maybe even another set after that."

"Does Claudio know about your big plans?" he teased.

"He knows," she confirmed. "We're just waiting for the okay from my doctor to start trying again."

He winced. "You just had a baby three weeks ago."

"After two years of trying to get pregnant," she reminded her brother. "And believe me, there was a lot of trying."

He winced again. "You do not need to tell me things like that. In fact, I beg you not to."

Lucy grinned at him, her usual good humor obviously restored, then turned to Erin, who'd been remarkably quiet since his return.

"Can I leave this here to dry?"

"Of course," Erin agreed.

Lucy glanced at her watch. "We're heading over to the pizzeria now to meet Claudio for dinner—and so Grandma Jo can get her daily baby fix."

"Too late," Kyle told her. "Joel and I just came from there."

Lucy rolled her eyes. "So Grandma Jo can get her daily *granddaughter* fix," she clarified. "Which is sweeter than a grandson fix, because little girls are made of sugar and spice and everything nice."

"Maybe most little girls," Kyle said. "But if Seraphina grows up to be anything like her mom…"

Now his sister's gaze narrowed, and he held up his hands in mock surrender.

"…she'll be a force to be reckoned with."

* * *

Erin was a little concerned that everything would change after the-day-before-Father's-Day, and she was unmistakably relieved when she and Kyle settled back into their usual routines of sharing parenting responsibilities. The only difference was that they were now sharing a bed, too, and that her baby's father was now the main reason she was losing sleep because she was discovering there were much more pleasurable ways to spend time in bed.

He hadn't proposed again, but he wasn't shy about dropping hints that warned her his focus was in that direction. And sometimes she let herself imagine the future they could have together, as a family, and she wanted that future so badly she ached.

As June gave way to July, Erin and Kyle continued to marvel over their baby's development. He was rolling over *all the time* now—sometimes starting on one side of the living room and ending up on the other. His daily menu had been expanded to include vegetables—he was *not* a fan of green beans—and his communication skills were starting to develop beyond just babbling and cooing. And he loved to laugh, so much so that he sometimes laughed at himself laughing.

It was a happy time for Erin, who felt certain that life would be perfect if they could just keep on the way they were going. The idyll lasted until the third Tuesday of the month. Erin had taken the day off to spend with Kyle and Joel, and when Kyle suggested a walk after lunch, she didn't hesitate to agree. Though the heat of summer was like a blanket over the town, their walks often took them by the ice cream window at Sweet Caroline's.

But today, Kyle turned in the opposite direction, away from Main Street.

"Where are we going?"

"For a walk," he said, as if that wasn't obvious.

"Usually when we walk, we walk that way," she said, pointing.

"We can go for ice cream later," he promised. "Now we need to go this way so we're not late."

"Late for what?" she asked.

"You ask a lot of questions," he remarked.

"Because I like to know what's going on."

"You'll find out soon enough."

"Now would be soon enough," she said, but held back the rest of her questions until they turned onto Larrea Drive and he stopped in front of a house with a For Sale sign stuck in the grass.

"Ohmygod—are you buying a house?"

"I'm thinking about it," he said. "Aside from the fact that real estate is always a good investment, this one has four bedrooms, three bathrooms, two fireplaces and a great backyard that Joel could play in, complete with sandbox and swing set."

"Why do you need four bedrooms?"

"Well, we don't right now, but—"

She held up a hand. "Wait a minute...did you say *we*?"

"I said *we*," he confirmed. "I only want the house if you and Joel are going to live in it with me."

"Moving in together...that's a big step."

"I'm hoping you'll take a bigger one and finally say yes to my proposal."

Erin was saved from having to reply by the arrival of the real estate agent.

"JJ Green," the man introduced himself.

He shook their hands with enthusiasm and ushered them into the house that he promised was perfect for a growing family. After the tour, JJ warned that the property was new on the market and not likely to be there for long, but he promised that if they weren't ready to make a decision, he'd keep his eyes open and let them know when other similar properties became available.

"What do you think?" Kyle asked, as they began to retrace their steps toward home.

"Four bedrooms is a lot," Erin noted.

"I figured we should have a dedicated guest room, for when your mom comes to visit again."

"Let's not encourage that," she said, making him laugh.

"And we'll need at least one more bedroom for Joel's little brother or sister," he continued his justification for the extra space.

It wasn't the first time he'd mentioned the possibility of having another child, but she couldn't let him continue to hope for something that wasn't going to happen—at least not with her.

And she had to tell him why.

"I made an appointment to have a tubal ligation."

Kyle stopped in the middle of the sidewalk, his smile fading. "What?"

"Well, I made an appointment with a gynecologist to talk about it," she clarified.

He was silent for a long minute, considering the implications of her revelation. "You want to have surgery to ensure you don't get pregnant again?"

She nodded. "I'm sorry."

"I don't want an apology," he said, moving forward again. "I want to understand where this is coming from."

"Anna called yesterday," she told him. "She's pregnant again."

"What does that have to do with anything?" he wondered aloud.

"Nicky's only seven months old and, in another seven months, she's going to have another baby."

"And she doesn't want another baby?" he guessed.

"No, she does," Erin admitted. "She's thrilled to be pregnant again, even if she didn't expect it to happen so soon. According to the doctor, she's incredibly fertile."

"And you think that means you might be, too."

"We used protection and I still got pregnant," she reminded him.

He nodded slowly.

"And I'm not sorry," she said. "But we got really lucky with him. He's a great baby…but I don't want to push my luck."

"You think you wouldn't love another baby as much," he realized.

"I don't know," she admitted.

And the not knowing was obviously causing her anguish.

He understood that the scars she carried from her mother's rejection ran deep and he had no intention of diminishing their importance. He could only imagine how difficult it had been for her, the distance between her and her mom, exacerbated by Anna's close bond with Bonnie. Considering all of that, it wasn't surprising she'd have concerns about the relationships she might develop with her own children.

"I love Joel more than I ever thought it was possible to love anyone," she confided to him now. "But I'm not sure I want to have another child."

He was silent for a long minute before responding, "If you're contemplating a surgical procedure, you need to be sure that you don't."

She nodded and brushed at the tears that spilled onto her cheeks.

They were both silent the rest of the way home, any interest in ice cream long forgotten.

"Were you going to tell me?" Kyle asked, when they'd returned to the privacy of her apartment. "Or was this surgery something else you planned to keep a secret?"

"Of course, I was going to tell you."

"Are we going to talk about it, then? Or have you already made up your mind?"

"I'd like to talk about it," she said.

"Because this doesn't just affect you," he said.

"I know."

"It affects us—you and me and Joel. Our family."

She nodded her agreement.

"And you dropped it like a bombshell. Out of the blue."

"You took me to look at a house. Out of the blue," she countered.

"Should I apologize for that?" he asked incredulously. "Was I wrong to think that we might want a home in which to build our life together?"

"No. You weren't wrong," she said. "But you caught me off guard. You always said you didn't plan to be a father, and suddenly you're talking about filling a four-bedroom house with kids."

"I mentioned the possibility of a brother or sister for Joel. One."

"The number isn't the issue," she said.

"What is the issue?"

"I'm scared," she admitted.

"It's okay to be scared," he told her. "But you don't have to be scared alone. I'm here for you, Erin. Please don't shut me out."

"I didn't mean to shut you out. I just need some time to figure things out."

Apparently Kyle needed some time, too, because he slept in his own apartment that night.

Erin didn't blame him for that. Just as she knew she wouldn't blame him if he decided that he wanted more than she was willing to give him. But she would be heartbroken.

"How was your appointment?" Kyle asked, when

she got home after seeing the doctor Thursday afternoon.

She immediately scooped up the baby, who was having tummy time on the floor, and sat him on her lap for a cuddle. Because she might have a lot of doubts about a lot of things, but the one thing she knew for certain was that she loved Joel with her whole heart.

"It was fine, I guess," she finally said in answer to the question. "But Doctor Alipio won't schedule surgery until I've talked to a counselor."

"How do you feel about that?" he asked cautiously.

"I don't think a few counseling sessions are going to change my mind, but I also think they're probably a good idea."

She smiled as Joel reached for the locket hanging around her neck. She'd worn it every day since Kyle had given it to her, but the baby's fascination with the shiny bauble had yet to wane.

"Can I go with you?"

Erin was surprised by the offer and immediately realized that she shouldn't have been. Because whether or not she decided to go ahead with the surgery, Kyle was right—her decision would affect not only her body but also their relationship and their family.

"You want to hear about the potential side effects, like depression, mood swings and loss of sex drive?" she asked, keeping her tone light so he wouldn't guess the extent of her own concerns about the possible repercussions of the surgery.

"I want to know what you know, so that we can make important decisions about our future together."

She nodded and reached for the ring of colorful plastic keys that Joel liked to shake—and chew on—in an effort to distract him from her locket, now firmly in his grasp. "You're right. And I think I would like you to be there when I talk to the counselor."

"Then I will be," he told her. "And if you decide that you're one hundred percent sure you don't want another baby but you're not sure about the surgery, it might make more sense for me to…um…deal with things on my end."

The comment was so shocking and unexpected, she completely forgot about the baby's viselike grip on her necklace for a moment. "Do you mean a vasectomy?"

He nodded, though she hadn't missed his instinctive wince when she said the word.

"I've been doing a little bit of research," he said. "And it seems there are a lot more risks for a woman with tubal ligation than for a man…getting snipped."

If the topic wasn't so serious, she might have smiled at his obvious discomfort in talking about the procedure.

"I don't think you really want to get snipped," she said.

"Well, no," he admitted. "But I really want you to know that I am one hundred percent committed to doing whatever needs to be done so that you'll finally agree to marry me."

He couldn't hear the word *vasectomy* without wincing, but he was willing to do it. *For her.*

She was touched and humbled and more than a little scared. "Are you sure that's what you want? That me and Joel would be enough for you?"

"I love you, Erin. You and Joel are everything to me. And I'm willing to do whatever it takes not only to prove that to you but to ensure you feel comfortable about living our life together in that fabulous house on Larrea Drive."

She finally managed to unfurl the baby's fingers from around the locket and turned him on her lap so that his back was to her front. She jiggled the keys again, and he immediately grabbed for them.

"More than once, you mentioned that Joel should have a brother or sister," she reminded him.

Kyle shrugged. "And then I remembered that sibling relationships aren't really all they're cracked up to be."

Of course, he was lying. She'd seen him with his siblings. Not just Lucy, but even Duncan, Callum and Fiona.

"I hate the idea of you giving up your dream of a big family for me."

"It was only a dream," he pointed out. "And a recent one at that. You and Joel are real, and you're everything that I need. You are my family."

He said the words with such intensity and conviction, she knew that he meant them.

But *what if,* somewhere down the road, he changed his mind?

What if he began to resent her for taking the choice away from him?

What if she stopped being afraid of the future and accepted everything he was offering her right now?

"I love you, Erin. Not because you're the mother of my child, but because you're you. And any decision about whether to have or not have another child isn't going to change the way I feel about you. I only ask that we make that decision together."

She realized then that it wasn't easy to let go of her fears, but it was the simplest thing in the world to open her heart to the man she loved and the possibilities for their future together.

"I love you, too, Kyle. You know that, don't you?"

"I know," he said with a small smile. "But I still like to hear you say it every now and then. Or all the time."

She smiled then, too. "I love you more than I could express if we had a hundred years together, but I'm still scared that I'm going to screw this up."

"You're not going to screw anything up, because there's no *you* or *me* anymore," he told her. "We're a team. Whatever choices need to be made, we'll make them together. Whatever the repercussions, we'll face them together. Okay?"

"Okay," she agreed, her heart suddenly feeling lighter, lifted by his love. "But there is one little snag in your plan."

"What's that?"

"I detoured by Larrea Drive on my way home," she confided, as she gently jiggled the baby. "I was hoping to reassure myself that the house wasn't as perfect as I remembered. But I was wrong… It was perfect. And now it's sold."

She didn't know how to explain the profound sense of disappointment she'd felt when she saw the SOLD sticker affixed to the For Sale sign, when she'd realized that her dream of living there with Kyle had barely had a chance to materialize before it was gone.

"I know it's sold," Kyle told her. "I bought it."

"You…what?" She didn't realize she'd stopped jiggling her leg until Joel started to squirm, prompting her to resume the rhythmic motion. "Why?"

"Because I decided it was going to be ours as soon as I saw your eyes light up when we walked into the master suite."

She remembered the walk-in closets, the full en suite bath and the sitting area with a gas fireplace. And she remembered how easy it had been to imagine making love with him in a king-size bed in that room while their son slept across the hall.

Still, she was stunned by his response. And perhaps a little wary. "Do you think that if we're living in that house, I'll change my mind about wanting to have another baby?"

"Do you think I'd buy a house in an effort to manipulate your feelings?"

"No," she realized, immediately chagrined that such a thought had even crossed her mind. "But it's a lot of house for just three people."

"It's the perfect house for *us*," he insisted. "You said so yourself."

"I did," she acknowledged, hugging the baby a little closer.

"Now…if I ask you to marry me again, will you say yes this time?"

Joel tipped his head back against her chest to look at her, as if he was waiting for her answer, too.

"What do you think?" she asked him. "Should I marry Daddy so that we can be a real family?"

"I know it's a little early for your first words, Joel," his dad said. "But if you could chime in here with a yes, I'd appreciate it."

The baby blew a raspberry.

Kyle sighed. "Not quite the endorsement I was hoping for." He shifted his gaze to Erin then. "It's going to have to be your call then."

"Well, you did once tell me that I should marry someone who knows how to cook," she reminded him. "And you definitely check that box."

His brows lifted. "Do I check any other boxes?"

"You're a fabulous father. You also have a great sense of humor and a kind heart, and you know how to rock my world, horizontally *and* vertically."

His lips curved. "Is that a yes?"

Joel answered with another raspberry, making both his parents laugh.

But Erin's expression quickly turned serious again and she lifted a hand to Kyle's cheek. "That's very definitely a yes," she said. "For now and forever."

Epilogue

"We should have done this in Haven," Erin remarked, as Kyle parked outside of the main house at Sunfish Resort. "We met in Haven. We live in Haven. Why wouldn't we get married in Haven?"

"Because it's traditional to get married in the bride's hometown," Kyle said, as he began pulling suitcases and various baby items out of the back of their rental vehicle. An SUV, of course, because when you traveled with a child, you needed a lot of stuff.

"I think the fact that our eight-and-a-half-month-old son is going to be our ring bearer is proof that we make our own traditions."

"And also because your mom asked," her soon-to-be husband reminded her. "Because she wanted the whole family to come together here in celebration."

Which Erin understood, because the last time they'd all been together was for her dad's funeral.

Six months later, so much had changed for all of them.

Anna and Nick and Nicky had moved into their own home, only a few miles down the road from the resort, leaving Bonnie on her own.

But not for long.

A few weeks later, she'd decided she wouldn't mind having a roommate. Coincidentally, Marissa's widowed mom, Luanne Harding, had moved to Silver Hook—and moved in with her daughter's family—making all of them a little crazy. Living at the resort allowed Luanne to be close enough to visit her grandkids whenever she wanted, but far enough away that she wasn't tripping over them every time she went to the kitchen to make a cup of tea.

Ian and Marissa continued to run the resort and were considering new offerings and packages to increase their off-season occupancy.

Owen and Roger had run into some roadblocks in their efforts to have a baby but had recently adopted two-year-old Maisy and three-year-old Libby and were happily tackling the challenges that came with being a family.

"Which we didn't anticipate would include seven and a half hours of connecting flights to get from Oregon to Arkansas for my sister's wedding," Owen grumbled, when Erin shared their plans.

"But we wouldn't miss it for the world," Roger promised.

Erin couldn't wait to meet her new nieces in person. And to give lots of love to Ella, Amie and Nicky, too.

She'd been both looking forward to and dreading this trip—her first time back since her dad's passing. Even planning the informal ceremony from a distance had made her heart ache, because she knew he wouldn't be there to walk her down the aisle or share the traditional father-daughter dance—or sneak away from the reception early to do some night fishing. And she'd worried that being in Silver Hook, at Sunfish Bay, would only make her more aware of her father's absence.

But as she breathed in the familiar pine scent and listened to the birds singing in the trees, she realized that her dad was there.

Every which way she turned, there were memories of him, surrounding and enveloping her. And she knew that this was exactly the right place to formalize the start of her new life, with the man she loved and the child they'd made together.

The ceremony, three days later, went off without a hitch.

The radiant bride carried a hand-tied bouquet of white calla lilies; the smiling groom held an eighteen-pound baby sporting a bow tie just like his daddy's.

Family and friends witnessed the exchange of vows and rings beneath clear blue skies, with the sun sparkling off the lake in the background and Brian Napper's beloved fishing boat tied up at the dock.

Afterward, there was plenty of food and drink for

the guests to enjoy as they mixed and mingled and passed babies around.

Bonnie had stolen Joel away from his parents at the first opportunity, wanting to spend as much time as possible with her grandson. Jo was currently helping Owen assemble plates of food for his daughters, while Roger chased the girls around the yard. Lucy had ducked into the house for some peace and quiet to nurse Seraphina, and Claudio and Nick could be overheard debating the merits of live bait fishing.

Erin watched as her baby was passed off to Marissa so that Grandma Bonnie could give some attention to Ella and Amie, then her own attention was snagged by Nicky, toddling across the grass, before zeroing in on Joel again.

"Look at that," Erin whispered, touching a hand to her husband's arm.

Kyle turned his head to follow the direction of her gaze.

Marissa had set Joel down for a minute to pour a glass of punch for Libby, but the baby had apparently decided he didn't want to suffer the indignity of being on his bottom.

"He's pulling himself up," Kyle realized.

She nodded.

Joel had been able to stand for a while now, holding on to the coffee table in their living room or the leg of a chair in their dining room, but he hadn't—until this moment—demonstrated the ability to pull himself into a standing position.

"Another beautiful memory to add to our perfect wedding day," Erin said, her eyes growing misty.

Until Kyle said, "Uh-oh."

"What?"

But her husband was already racing toward their son, who was starting to wobble on his feet, both of his hands still clutching the fabric draped over the cake table.

Erin watched in horror as the baby started to fall, taking the cloth—and three-layers of exquisitely decorated pink champagne cake—with him.

Kyle pulled the baby out of harm's way just as the cake hit the ground.

There were gasps of shock mixed with a few stifled giggles.

The shock of being unceremoniously yanked, even into his beloved daddy's embrace, made Joel's lower lip wobble and his blue eyes fill with tears.

"Ohmygod." Marissa looked from the cake carnage on the ground to the bride, her expression stricken. "I'm so sorry. I only turned my back for a second."

"And that's why it's important to babyproof," Kyle said.

Erin laughed.

She couldn't help it.

While her sister and sister-in-law frantically tried to salvage at least part of the cake, she heard Luanne ask, "Who wants ice cream?"

"Cake," Libby said, filling both hands with the pink confection.

"Cake," Maisy agreed, following her sister's example.

Then Ella and Amie were there, too, determined to get their share.

Kyle handed their teary-eyed son to his mommy.

Erin wiped a smear of frosting off Joel's cheek, then let him suck the sugary treat off her finger. He smiled through his tears, happy to discover a new—and delicious—food.

As the bride hugged the baby close, she felt the groom's arms come around her.

"You were saying something about our perfect wedding day?" he reminded her.

"Maybe not perfect," she allowed, tipping her head back against his shoulder, "but certainly unforgettable."

* * * * *

Look for Devin Blake's story,
the next installment in
Brenda Harlen's miniseries,
Match Made in Haven,
coming soon to Harlequin Special Edition!

#2857 THE MOST ELIGIBLE COWBOY
Montana Mavericks: The Real Cowboys of Bronco Heights
by Melissa Senate

Brandon Taylor has zero interest in tying the knot—until his unexpected fling with ex-girlfriend Cassidy Ware. Now she's pregnant—but Cassidy is not jumping at his practical proposal. She remembers their high school romance all too well, and she won't wed without proof that Brandon 2.0 can be the *real* husband she longs for.

#2858 THE LATE BLOOMER'S ROAD TO LOVE
Matchmaking Mamas • by Marie Ferrarella

When other girls her age were dating and finding love, Rachel Fenelli was keeping the family restaurant going after her father's heart attack. Now she's on the verge of starting the life she should have started years ago. Enter Wyatt Watson, the only physical therapist her stubborn dad will tolerate. But little does Rachel know that her dad has an ulterior—matchmaking?—motive!

#2859 THE PUPPY PROBLEM
Paradise Pets • by Katie Meyer

There's nothing single mom Megan Palmer wouldn't do to help her son, Owen. So when his school tries to keep his autism service dog out of the classroom, Megan goes straight to the principal's office—and meets Luke Wright. He's impressed by her, and the more they work together, the more he hopes to win her over...

#2860 A DELICIOUS DILEMMA
by Sera Taíno

Val Navarro knew she shouldn't go dancing right after a bad breakup and she definitely shouldn't be thinking the handsome, sensitive stranger she meets could be more than a rebound. Especially after she finds out his father's company could shut down her Puerto Rican restaurant and unravel her tight-knit neighborhood. Is following her heart a recipe for disaster?

#2861 LAST-CHANCE MARRIAGE RESCUE
Top Dog Dude Ranch • by Catherine Mann

Nina and Douglas Archer are on the verge of divorce, but they're both determined to keep it together for one last family vacation, planned by their ten-year-old twins. And when they do, they're surprised to find themselves giving in to the romance of it all. Still, Nina knows she needs an emotionally available husband. Will a once-in-a-lifetime trip show them the way back to each other?

#2862 THE FAMILY SHE DIDN'T EXPECT
The Culhanes of Cedar River • by Helen Lacey

Marnie Jackson has one mission: to discover her roots in Cedar River. She's determined to fulfill her mother's dying wish, but her sexy landlord and his charming daughters turn out to be a surprising distraction from her goal. Widower Joss Culhane has been focusing on work, his kids and his own family drama. Why risk opening his heart to another woman who might leave them?

She returned with the pot of melted chocolate and poured
the now-cooled liquid into a cup, handing it to him. Val
fussing over him made him feel positively giddy. He raised
the cup and took a sip. Chocolate and nutmeg melted on his
tongue, sending a surge of pleasure through him.

"Puerto Rican hot chocolate," she said, taking her seat
again. "Maybe the sugar will perk you up."

"You're worried about me falling asleep at the wheel."

"This is how I'm made. I'm a worrier."

His eyes flickered to her strong hands, admiring the signs
of use, and he wondered at what other things she created
with them. "No one's worried about me in a very long time."

He was learning to read her, so he was ready for her
zinger. "In my family, worrying is an Olympic sport, so
if you ever need someone to worry about you, feel free to
borrow any of us."

He smiled into his cup. "I appreciate the offer."

She settled onto the stool, shuffling her feet into and out of her Crocs. "I wasn't really looking for anything tonight."

"Neither was I. But here we are."

Her eyes flicked away again, a habit he was beginning to understand was a nervous reaction, as if she might find the answer to her confusion somewhere in her environment. "That breakup I told you about? That was the last time I've been with anyone."

"Same. It's been a while for me, too." Maybe too long, if his complete lack of confidence right now was any indication.

"Just managing expectations." She poked at her cake, swirling the fork in the fragrant cream. "I'm really not up for anything serious."

"That's fair."

She took a bite, chewing slowly, the gears of her mind visibly working. He didn't rush her, and his patience was rewarded when, after a full minute, she said, "Okay. Next Saturday. I don't work Sundays."

"What if I can't wait until next Saturday?"

"It's like that?" she whispered.

"It's like that," he answered, and she was suddenly so close that if he leaned forward, it would be impossibly easy to kiss her. And he wanted to kiss her badly; the wanting burned hot in his chest. But he couldn't. It would be a lie.

Don't miss
A Delicious Dilemma *by Sera Taíno,*
available September 2021 wherever
Harlequin Special Edition books and ebooks are sold.

Harlequin.com